I0681878

Produced by David Carner
Copyright © 2013 by David Carner
Cover design by R. Carner

Paperback ISBN: 978-0-9859514-9-8

To find out more about John Fowler, please feel free to follow my author page on Facebook. The David Carner fan page currently holds all announcements pertaining to this series. Also check out www.davidcarner.com for information on this series and any other works. You may also follow me on twitter @davidcarner.

Other Works

Bad Day in Queen's Landing

The John Fowler Novels

The Road to Justice

Sins of the Son

This Thing of Ours

Journey's End

Day's Past

Cold Revenge

The Fall of the Cabal (Coming Christmas 2016)

Evil Incorporated (Coming Christmas 2018)

Never Say Never(Coming Christmas 2020)

Check out http://david-carner.blogspot.com/ for my current free short story, Bad Day in Queen's Landing and any other Queen's Landing stories.

Chapter 1

Dwayne Sapp stood in front of his bathroom mirror. He stared at his reflection. He saw a pathetic, brown haired, shirtless man wearing only pajama bottoms looking back at him. He didn't recognize himself any longer.

"Hurry up in there, sweetie," the voice from the other room called out. Dwayne gritted his teeth. That voice had turned him into the thing in the mirror he despised. He had been married for five years now, but he had had enough. Liz had put her nose into his business one too many times. Dwayne had done everything he could to tell her he needed his space, but she refused to listen. They had to do everything together, she kept insisting. Liz didn't get that sometimes he needed space, and he was going to get it - one way or another. Dwayne looked down at the knife in front of him. He used to have 50 of them; now he had 22, and after tonight, if everything went right, he was going to have 21. Dwayne took the knife and held it behind his back. He turned out the light in the bathroom and opened the bathroom door. The lights were out in the bedroom. He stood there for a minute to let his eyes adjust to the darkness. He stared at his wife who was lying in bed, wearing a negligee. Her blond hair shimmered in the moonlight; that made him feel at ease. The sight of her reminded him why he had picked her in the first place.

"Come here, baby," she said. Dwayne smiled a sinister smile and started toward her. He pulled the knife from behind his back. He wanted her to know; he wanted her to be scared and understand he had no choice in what he had to do. Liz saw the knife and sighed. She reached under the pillow and pulled out her pistol. Dwayne looked at her and took another step. A red light shot out of the gun, landing in the middle of his forehead. Dwayne stopped mid-stride.

"You're going to shoot me with the gun I gave you?" he asked in surprise.

"You got rid of my other one," she responded with a sad smile on her face.

"I had too," Dwayne said, more frustrated that she still blamed him for getting rid of her gun than the fact the gun was trained on him.

"Oh, Dwayne," she said with the laser light still pointed toward his skull. "I had so hoped those sessions with the marriage counselor would have helped."

"That would be kind of hard since you killed the first one because he disagreed with you," he rebutted. Liz looked at him with disdain.

"You know he just sided with you because you're a man," she rebuked. She sighed. "I don't see any other way out of this. Do you?" Dwayne shook his head. He hadn't wanted it to come to this, but he knew either they went through with this, or they would remain married, and both of them would be miserable. Dwayne walked over to the chair in the room and sat down with his head in his hands. Liz lowered the gun.

"Do you want to say it, or me?" he asked. Liz gave him a sad smile.

"Dwayne, I want a divorce."

John Fowler
New York, New York

Chapter 2

John looked around the bar. He was back in This Thing of Ours and was trying to figure out why he was there again. John came around the corner of the bar and saw Sam's ring lying on the ground. He bent down and picked it up. As he examined it, he saw something move on the far side of the bar out of the corner of his eye. John drew his weapon and slowly made his way toward the movement. John stopped as he got to where he could make out the form on the ground. There lay Chet, blood coming out of his mouth.

"We missed something, Boss," Chet said weakly. John stared at him in horror.

"Why don't you just put him out of his misery?" Bruce's voice said. John spun around, expecting to see Bruce behind him. No one was there, and when John turned back around, Chet wasn't there either.

"This is all in my mind," John muttered.

"Is it?" Bruce's voice asked. "Hehehehe," the mad laughter carried through the bar. John turned around and tried to locate the voice, when he noticed movement behind the bar. John knelt and aimed his gun where he saw the movement. He saw the shape again and fired three shots, center mass.

"What I should have done the first time," John said, regretting he hadn't killed Bruce in the past. John carefully approached the bar, looked over, and gasped.

"Jess!" he yelled. John had put three bullets into Jessica. She lay there, a look of shock on her face. Laughter filled the establishment as John vaulted over the bar. He took Jessica in his arms, almost the same way she had held him when Bruce had shot him. Laughter continued to roll through the bar.

John took his eyes off Jessica for a second and scanned around to see if he could find Bruce anywhere. When he looked back down, Jessica was gone.

"This is a dream," John said, standing and trying to wake himself up.

"It's your nightmare, buddy," Bruce's voice said from behind him. John began to turn when he felt the bullet rip through him.

"NOOOOOOO!" John screamed, sitting straight up in bed. As he shot up, his right hand planted and pushed off Jessica's shoulder. Jessica, surprised by being awakened, grabbed the hand that was holding her down and twisted it, putting John in a MMA move known as an arm bar.

"OWWWWW!" John screamed in physical pain. Jessica realized that she had John and let him go. Jessica started to apologize when she got a good look at John. He was sweat covered, he was breathing like he was about to hyperventilate, and he was looking around in a panic. Jessica wasn't sure his mind was really in the room.

"John, snap out of it," she said. John stared at her blankly. Jessica reached back and slapped him across the face, trying to bring him out of shock. John's eyes narrowed, and it was quickly apparent to Jessica that he now knew where he was.

"Do you mind not beating me to a pulp?" he asked, still a little wild eyed.

"Another nightmare," she said, not asked. John nodded.

"Yeah," John replied, a little sullenly. "I was at the circus surrounded by clowns."

"That's not your 'scared of clowns' reaction," Jessica said. "You would be in the corner sucking your thumb if it were clowns." John stared at Jessica, and the emotion overwhelmed him. He began to laugh. Jessica couldn't help herself and joined in. They laughed for a few minutes, and John finally caught his breath. "Bruce?" she asked quietly, holding his hand. John looked down at her hand and then back to her, nodding.

"Yeah," John replied. "Chet was dead, then I shot you by accident, and then Bruce shot me in the back, again."

"Excuse me? You shot me?"

"Can we not make this about you for once?"

"Uh, you shot me! How is this not about me?"

"It was a nightmare," John replied.

"You know what's going to be a nightmare? You explaining to Trip why you have two black eyes in the morning," Jessica countered. John smiled, and Jessica rubbed his hand. She laid her head on his shoulder. "Are you sure you're ready?" John shook his head.

"No," John replied honestly. "But, I've got to try."

"Just don't shoot anyone," Jessica said. John moved forward quickly, causing Jessica to fall back onto the bed. She reached up and grabbed him in a hug from behind, her fingers tracing the bullet wound on his chest. John stared down at it and wondered if he would ever be ready to return. He exhaled and pushed all the worry from his mind. John had a job to finish, and Bruce wasn't going to stop him. Well, not unless he shot John again.

Chapter 3

Chet was by himself with the music blasting out of his computer. Chet wondered what John would say if he saw Chet using this state of the art computer to be nothing more than a souped-up radio station? John always said that Chet was a computer genius. He probably could have been a rich computer tycoon or a world class hacker . . . or both. Chet didn't know if he agreed with that, but he knew a few things when it came to computers.

Chet was enjoying the music, and let it wash over him. He liked all different types of music, but he had started to grow tired of 80s music. It wasn't that he didn't like it, but when John was around and he was allowed to play music without headphones, it had to be from the 80s. Chet wondered why John loved the music from that decade so much.

Chet started to think back to the events of the past few months. It just seemed like yesterday that Chet had knocked on John's door, asking John to help the FBI. That case had led to more than Chet had dared to dream.

John had been reunited with his team Jessica and Chet, and they were once again under the command of Trip. It was supposed to be a one-time thing, at least that's what John had been told. John was only supposed to be a consultant on the case. The team had solved what seemed to be a quadruple homicide that turned out to be so much more. Chet smiled as he thought of the history they had made by making the President resign because of what they had exposed the First Lady of being involved in over twenty-five years prior. He shook his head and laughed.

After that, John had been reinstated into the FBI, and the team's first official case was to help John's constant nemesis find his kidnapped father. Of course, what none of them knew was that his nemesis, Bruce, was the man who had killed John's wife Sam and caused John to leave the FBI some three years earlier. During all of this, John had also made up with many of the people he had insulted or distanced himself from during his alcoholism.

All of that had led to John confronting Bruce, and both men shooting the other, which led to Trip and the rest of the team faking John's death. Chet still wasn't sure that was the best move, but in the end, it helped bring Archibald Staples to justice. During that time, Ron had been introduced to the team and had begun helping Chet with his marksmanship.

John was supposed to take it easy for a few weeks. Chet wasn't sure that taking it easy meant getting married, but that's what John had done. Chet chuckled at the thought of the wedding. John's and Jessica's romance had been one of many years and a whirlwind at the same time. With the rest of his time off, the team had convinced John to write a book telling of their first case together, warts and all. John had finished it, and today was supposed to be the day that he returned to the FBI, but Chet was getting worried. Chet expected John to be the first one here, and he was nowhere to be seen.

"Hey!" came the voice from behind him. Chet spun around, pulled out of his thoughts, to see Ron and Jessica standing in the doorway, smiling. Chet turned down the music.

"Sorry about that," Chet said. Jessica gave Chet a knowing smile. She knew exactly why Chet had the music cranked. If her husband had his way, things would fall right back into their same old pattern as soon as he showed up. Husband - Jessica still couldn't get over the fact that she and John were married. To say that the two of them got off to a rocky start was a tremendous understatement. Over the years they worked together, they had fought like cats and dogs while fighting something within themselves.

Jessica often wondered if their story didn't belong on one of those daytime TV talk shows where the audience was always chanting the host's name. John had been married to Sam when Jessica and John first worked together. Sam and Jessica had become instant best friends, and John and Jessica, they had become…Jessica didn't know if there was a term that could describe what they had become. Jessica couldn't stand John, and John felt the same way about Jessica except there was something that each one felt toward the other that made no real sense. To make things even crazier, Sam knew how both felt about the other one.

As if all of that wasn't enough, each person knew that the other one was not going to act on their feelings. John had this code he followed - something obviously derived from an extinct, ancient cult of ninjas that only John knew the secrets to. Jessica knew John would never act on his feelings for Jessica, which made her admire him even more. Jessica would never hurt Sam, and Sam knew it. When Sam died, Jessica was heartbroken and full of hope all at the same time. It wasn't long until she was only heartbroken though. Jessica was put in charge of interrogating John after the explosion that everyone had thought killed Sam. John had been sure Sam's death was all his fault, and he lashed out at everyone around him. For three years, he and Jessica didn't speak.

All that was behind them now; today was going to be an interesting day. Today was the day John returned to the FBI, again.

"Where's John?" Chet asked.

"Yeah, where is he?" Ron echoed. Ron was the newest member of the team. He had joined after John had been shot by Bruce. John knew Ron wanted to be in New York for some reason, and John wanted Ron nearby in case he suffered any side effects from being shot. John had shown some minor signs of suffering from PTSD.

"He's here," Jessica said, smiling. "He's coming back, as only John can."

Chapter 4

Director Lionel Pennyworth Smothers III, known to everyone in the building, at his insistence, as Trip, walked down the hall. There was an open folder that he was reading in one hand, a cup of coffee in the other. He closed the file and wished he could erase the contents from his mind. The folder was on former FBI agent, Bruce Cosby. Bruce was the son of one time senator, and now Vice-President of the United States, Jeremiah Cosby. Jeremiah was a man who fought to end political corruption. Apparently, someone in the FBI did not get the memo and hired his son, thinking there would be some type of quid pro quo in return. Trip had also discovered in the last little bit that Bruce's psychological profile had been falsified because in Trip's world, Bruce was just stone-cold crazy. Trip knew that wasn't the proper term or the politically correct term, but after dealing with Bruce as long as he had and dealing with the fallout of Bruce shooting John, that was the nicest thing Trip could say about Bruce.

Trip chuckled to himself. There was a time he was known in the agency as "By The Book Lionel." Some might still think of him that way, but what they didn't know when it came to John's team would destroy that image. John's team had come about due to some wrangling by then Senator Cosby. He believed that there needed to be a watchdog group, for a lack of a better term, that could investigate things they thought were a risk to national security. Trip's team had Homeland Security and FBI clearance, and if pressed, he suspected they might be able to get some CIA clearance, but to date, they had never needed to. Trip jotted that down in the back of his mind; he might need that clearance at some point to strengthen a case they had been working on.

Over the years, John and Trip had butted heads, but for the most part, it had only been because Trip was trying to protect John. Trip didn't know how John did what he did, but no one was as good of an investigator as John Fowler was. John had this ability to watch someone as they talked and read their body for clues. John was a human lie detector machine in layman's terms. There were some people John couldn't read because they didn't feel guilt, and their bodies gave off no clues. Bruce had been one of those people.

After John had gone undercover, watched a FBI agent die, and was forced to cover it up as part of his undercover work, John couldn't deal with his emotions. John saw things as black and white. There were no shades of gray with him. This was the root of many of John's problems. When having a conversation with someone John said what he thought whether it was the right thing to say or not. John had his own list of rules, and all of them seemed to contradict each other. Trip had learned the rules over the years. John would never tell you a direct lie if he could help it. They almost made him break out in hives. That being said, you had better watch the phrasing of your question or his answer. John didn't break his word, or kill, but anything other than that, was someone else's law, and not John's. Trip often wondered how John could work at a job that was law enforcement when he didn't agree with so many of them.

Trip thought for a second about Mark Glass, the FBI agent that had been killed in front of John. John had to remain undercover, and to deaden the pain and his inability to enact justice due to his assignment, John began to drink. John was becoming deeply entrenched in the mob, and John had already been drinking with them on multiple social occasions. Mark's death sent him to a whole new level of drinking. The mob believed John was ostracized by the FBI, and when John covered up Mark's death for them, he was in. John was in so deep when the arrests were finally made, more than 50 top level mob members were taken off the street, none of which have returned to this day.

Trip had to admit that working with John was one of the true joys of his job and also some of the worst parts of his job. Trip knew John couldn't work with just anyone, and there were times he let John go a little further than he should, but John never crossed the line. He would run all the way up to it, put his toe on it, but he didn't cross it. Trip realized he was at his office door. He started to go in when the sight in front of him made him stop dead in his tracks.

Chapter 5

Trip stared into his office. Someone was sitting in his chair, at his desk, feet propped up, and looking like he owned the place.

"Miss me?" John asked. The brim of the hat he was wearing was at such a low angle that it nearly covered his eyes.

"What exactly do you think you're doing?" Trip asked. John smiled.

"I'm getting reinstated today," John replied. "Or, I'm getting dragged out of here by security." Trip considered the second option for a second. As much as he would enjoy seeing John thrown out of the building, there was no real reason to do so. In fact, Trip had pushed the time off a week longer than he ever thought he could. Trip dug through the files that were in his arms, picked one, and flung it onto his desk. John picked it up, looked at it, took his feet off the desk, and hopped out of the chair.

"It's already cleared?" John asked.

"Yep," Trip replied. "Now if the famous author doesn't mind, I have work to do." John groaned at the dig. Trip, Jeremiah, and Jessica had convinced John to write a book, telling the first adventure of John and his team. John thought it was just something to keep him busy. Jessica sent it to an agent who loved it and sent it on to a publishing house. In six weeks, John's novel was to be published. John decided to be difficult. Well, he was normally difficult. He decided to be extra difficult. He sat in the chair, staring at Trip. Trip sighed and pulled out another file.

"I didn't really want to deal with this right now, but..." he said as he pulled out a file from the stack in his arm and tossed it on the desk to John. "I think this is what you're wanting." John grabbed the file and began to flip through it. He looked up at Trip when he found what he was looking for. Tears were in John's eyes. Trip nodded, understanding. Over the past few weeks, Jessica and John had been seeing someone that resembled John's dead wife, Samantha. John finally confronted the girl, Amanda, and she had spit in his face. John had the saliva tested to compare Amanda's DNA against Sam's. There was no doubt; Amanda was Sam's daughter. John looked down at and continued to flip though the file. A frustrated look crossed his face. He looked up at Trip. Trip was looking away, knowing what was coming.

"What does 'unknown donor' mean?" John asked. Trip turned back to John.

"It means that they don't know who the donor is," Trip answered, knowing such an answer was going to drive John crazy. John glared at Trip, which was something new. In the old days, Trip would have enjoyed getting one over on John, but not today. Not with this case. This case hit too close to John for Trip's comfort. When it came to things that had to do with Sam, John was almost uncontrollable. Trip took a deep breath and gave the same answer he was given. "There was nothing in any database they searched."

"You're talking about whatever general database they track DNA with?" John asked. Trip nodded. "It needs to be checked against the DNA of the Presidents." Trip winced and took a deep breath. This wasn't going to be fun.

"Three things," Trip began. "Who's to say that such a database exists? If it did, you don't have a lot of friends that would go out on a limb for you on this one, especially the secret service, so who's going to approve this?" Trip paused.

"That's just two," John said, thinking he knew what the third thing was. Trip nodded.

"Let's say you're right about whom the DNA belongs to," Trip said, gauging John's reaction. John sat, stoically. "Can you handle it?"

"One, how can such a database not exist?" John asked. Trip had to give him that one. "Two, we both know who I can ask." Trip again had to admit he knew the answer to that one as well. "And three…" John paused and gathered himself. He stood up, straightened his coat, and looked Trip right in the eye. "Doesn't she deserve it?"

"Who?" Trip asked. "Sam, Amanda, or Jessica?" John wasn't expecting Jessica to be on that list but knew Trip was right. For all the craziness that had been the weird triangle between Jessica, Sam, and John, John knew that Jessica wanted what was best for her best friend's daughter.

"Yes," John answered quietly. Trip looked away for a second. This discussion was dragging up old feelings of guilt for everyone. There wasn't a person on John's team or associated with the case that didn't think Sam's death wasn't his or her fault. Trip, with an unfamiliar grin, looked back at John.

"I'll see what I can do," Trip said. John chuckled and shook his head.

"I get now why that grin makes everyone so irritated," John answered as he moved out from behind Trip's desk. John sat down in a chair across from Trip as Trip took his seat. Trip turned to look at his agent.

"Is there something else?" Trip asked. John chuckled, got up, and headed to the door.

"It's good to be back," John said, pausing at the door. Trip didn't answer, and John left.

"It's good to have you back," Trip said quietly to an empty office. John stuck his head back in, grinning.

"I heard that," John said as he raced out before Trip could react. Trip shook his head. Things were never calm with John around.

Chapter 6

John headed down the hall, proud of himself. He had accomplished everything he had hoped to when he walked back into the FBI earlier this year. John chuckled to himself. When he walked in, he was a private investigator that was just going to consult on a case to have a chance to look at his wife's murder file. Now, he had found out not only who had killed his wife but why Bruce had done so. The problem was John knew that while Archibald's little evil cabal wasn't directly behind his wife's death, they were involved. John felt it was time to bring all of them down.

Archibald was sitting in a prison cell, rotting right now, but John wouldn't rest until he brought down the other two suspected members. The group mostly agreed that Duck was one of the members. John had to convince them that the other member was Kenneth Nichols. John wasn't as tech savvy as most, but he didn't think it was an accident that the number Archibald called when John confronted him before he was shot went to a cell phone in the White House.

John pulled himself from his thoughts as he walked into the foxhole. John looked around the room. Chet was at his computer doing who knows what. Ron had a desk sent down to the foxhole to work on since he had been assigned to the group. John glanced over to the two offices on the far side. The two offices had glass windows that looked into the large room. His office was empty, his, and the other had the other three members of the group in it, talking about something. John grinned and headed over to them. Halfway across the room, Chet saw him.

"Boss!" Chet exclaimed. "You're cleared?" John pulled out his reinstatement papers, and Chet clapped his hands together. He turned toward Jessica who put a finger over his mouth before he could speak.

"For the love of God," she began. "Please don't say we're putting the band back together." From the look on Chet's face, it was obvious that was exactly what he was going to say. John shook his head and headed into his office. He looked around at the very Spartan set-up.

"Do I need a picture or something in here?" he asked aloud.

"You could, or you could just watch me," Jessica replied. John turned around, smiling.

"I wouldn't want to get a call from human resources about inappropriate behavior," John replied.

"Since when?" Jessica asked seriously. John just grinned. The smile left Jessica's face. "Did Trip tell you about the DNA sample?" John handed the file to Jessica. She looked at it and then back at John, a slow grin was growing across her face. John really didn't like these grins being used against him.

"You knew?" he asked. Jessica's grin just grew. "You knew, and you didn't tell me?" John really wasn't liking these grins.

"I was sworn to secrecy," she replied matter-of-factly. John shook his head.

"You're supposed to be loyal to me," John said. Jessica gave him the look. John didn't really know how to describe the look except he had never seen it before he married Sam. He didn't even know Jessica had the same look until after they were married. He supposed it was something taught to women in secret.

"Ouch," Ron said, standing in the doorway to John's office.

"So, you can see it too?" John asked. Ron nodded, not sure what John meant. John nodded, thinking. "Then, it's not something that only married men can see." Jessica shook her head and thought about asking what he meant but decided against it.

"Yeah," Ron said, not really sure what was going on. "I took this message for you," he said, handing John the message and hurrying off. Ron was wondering if this is what Trip meant when he told Ron be careful what you asked for.

"Does my phone not work?" John asked.

"Yeah, but everyone's been calling the main line down here instead of your office since you were out," Jessica replied. John looked a little irritated. "Are you afraid someone might hear something they shouldn't?" she asked, a little mockingly. John looked back at her and shook his head.

"You mock me, but you know, sometimes I hear very sensitive things that others don't have clearance to hear," John responded seriously. Jessica shook her head.

"Don't," she said. "Just don't."

"You think I'm joking, but I'm serious," John said. Ron couldn't help overhearing bits of the conversation and wondered if he wasn't trusted. He started to get up and head toward John's office when Chet appeared in front of him shaking his head.

"It's not you," Chet said. "Trust me. Don't get involved." Ron looked over at the two. Jessica looked like she was hearing the craziest thing in the world, and John looked as serious as one can look. Ron was catching words here and there, but he couldn't be hearing what he thought he was hearing. He turned to Chet who was shaking his head with his eyes closed. When Chet opened them, he saw the look on Ron's face and decided to explain.

"You know that comic book where the hero has the signal the police shine into the clouds to let him know that he's needed?" Chet asked. Ron nodded, scared where this was going. "John wants one for himself," Chet admitted. Ron, in total shock, looked at Chet and saw that he was serious. He looked over at John who was obviously arguing for this signal and Jessica who looked like she wanted to strangle John. Ron wondered if it was wise to ask John for his help. He obviously lived in a fantasy world, and what Ron needed John for was too important. Ron was going to keep this to himself for now. If he saw John was the man who could help him, he would talk to him. Ron looked at John again and didn't think that day would ever come.

Chapter 7

"Ron," John called over to Ron. Ron headed over to John.

"Hear him out," Chet whispered, following behind Ron. "I'm not saying he's right. You just have to listen to him. It's easier that way." Ron gave Chet a look. What kind of madness was this place?

"You're a fair and impartial judge," John began. Ron didn't necessarily agree with that statement. "If there was a signal to contact me, I think it would increase security and expediency." Ron just stared at John. John took the look as a signal to go on. "You had to take a message for me. If I had a big signal, I could go meet someone and talk to them discreetly. What do you think? They think I'm crazy." John had a very proud look on his face.

"Don't you think if the signal was in the sky that the person you're trying to keep your meeting secret from could follow the light in the sky back to the origin point?" Chet asked. The proud look fell off John's face as he turned toward Chet.

"I never considered that," John said softly, thinking of the implications. Ron shook his head.

"I have to agree with Chet," Ron said. John was nodding.

"So do I, now," John admitted. Ron didn't know what to think.

"Just say it, Ron," Jessica said, studying Ron.

"Why would you take something out of a comic book to use in trying to solve cases?" Ron asked, fearing the answer.

"Why wouldn't you?" John asked. He walked over to his bookshelf and pulled the one book that was on it and handed it to Ron. Ron looked at it.

"Sir Arthur Conan Doyle," Ron said. "A great writer."

"The first, and best, mystery writer of all time," John corrected. Ron shrugged. "Some would argue that," John added. "Just because he's only a writer doesn't mean he didn't have great ideas. Why do I care where a great idea comes from as long as it helps me solve a case?" Ron thought about what John said. "What if I learn something from a cooking show, but in one case, just one case, it helps me solve the case? I have a tool box, and I fill it with every tool I can. I may only use that tool once in my life, but if it helps solve a case, who cares?"

"You're serious," Ron said, not asked. John nodded.

"The name of this game is solving crimes, not worrying about who had the idea that cracked the case," John said. He looked at Jessica and then Chet. "These two bring their own special skill sets to the game, but do you think Chet is going to care for a minute if I unlock a computer that has the password as password because he was trying to do something too complex?" Chet shook his head. "Do you think Jessica is going to care if I crack someone in the interrogation room?" John stopped, thought, and added. "Well, now she wouldn't, but back then . . ." he trailed off as he shrugged his shoulders and smiled. Jessica laughed and put her hand on his shoulder.

"And do you think that John cares if we solved fifteen cases while he was out recovering from a bullet wound?" she asked with an evil grin on her face. John turned toward her, mouthing, "Fifteen?" She smiled at him. John shook his head and turned back to Ron.

"Anyway," John continued. "I'm always filing things away in my head that might be useful. They might not be, but you never know what random fact, idea, or hunch will break a case. Ninety-nine percent of cases are solved off good old-fashioned police work, but sometimes, you need something else." Ron nodded, reassessing his earlier thoughts about John. In fact, now he thought John might be the person he needed to help him. John would bring ideas and thoughts that had never been used before. Ron had to think. He headed back to his desk as John watched him.

Wheels were spinning in John's head. He didn't know why, but something changed with Ron during their talk. Well, it was more accurate to say John talking at Ron. Something was up with Ron, and John wasn't sure what it was. John glanced down at the message Ron had given him and decided that could wait until later. Right now, he had a different phone call to make.

Chapter 8

John dialed a number and waited for someone to pick up on the other end.

"This is John Fowler," he said into the phone. He was placed on hold. John put his hand over the receiver and mouthed to Jessica, "I'm on hold."

"Are they playing any of your favorite hits?" Jessica asked.

"No," John replied, looking a little disgusted. "It's talk radio and not good talk radio."

"There's good talk radio?" Jessica asked, wondering how she could ever forget about some of the lunacy that took place in the office when John was around.

"Sports talk," John replied a little insistently.

"I could do a sports talk show," Jessica replied, deciding it had been a while since she had riled him up, and she could use the fun.

"No one wants to hear about MMA fighting!" John exclaimed.

"Well, ma'boy, if you knew your wife a little better, you would know she does," the voice on the other end of the phone said. John nearly dropped the phone from the surprise. Jessica laughed and left John to talk.

"Sorry about that, sir," John said hastily. "I need a favor."

"Well spit it out, ma'boy, I'm not getting any younger," Vice-President Jeremiah Cosby replied.

"I need clearance to get into the DNA database of past presidents to run a comparison," John said. There was silence on the line. John was a little surprised. He figured this would be a quick call.

"May I ask why?" Jeremiah asked, his voice strange.

"I haven't told you, have I?" John said. "I'm an idiot, sir."

"Your beautiful bride has kept me in the loop, son, so just calm yourself," Jeremiah said. "I know about the lady you two keep seeing. I believe Amanda is her name."

"She's Sam's daughter, sir," John said, a little choked up.

"I see," Jeremiah replied. "The father?"

"That's why I need access to the database. I have reason to believe that former President Kenneth Nichols is the father. But, you already suspected that, didn't you?" John asked. He knew he shouldn't do his friend this way, but John had a suspicion that Jeremiah had known this for some time. There was no immediate response on the line. "Sir?"

"I'm here, boy," Jeremiah replied, a little miffed. "How long have you suspected? About me, I mean?"

"Since before I got shot," John replied.

"Tarnation, boy! I should take you on some of these negotiations I have to go to. You and your little ability would save me a tremendous amount of time!"

"You're avoiding the question, sir," John reminded Jeremiah.

"And persistent as a hungry bull dog at a meat factory," Jeremiah replied. John looked at the phone. He wasn't sure what that meant. Jeremiah continued. "I'll let you have the access if you'll agree to something for me."

"Name it," John said, feeling the old grin starting to grow across his face.

"Knock that grin off your face, and meet me at the Watergate Apartments later tonight," Jeremiah said grumpily. John couldn't believe he had been busted. "I'll contact you later with the exact time."

"See you then, sir," John responded. The line disconnected, and John stared at the phone for a second. He wasn't for sure what was going on, and he didn't like it.

Chapter 9

"Something wrong?" Jessica asked, pulling John from his thoughts. She had stuck her head in the office after she watched him sitting there for a few minutes. John hung up the phone which was making an annoying sound. He thought for a second.

"Jeremiah suspected that Kenneth Nichols was Amanda's father," John said, wanting to see Jessica's reaction. Jessica thought for a minute. "I'm really beginning to think our ex-president is more involved in the cabal."

"You just like saying cabal," Jessica accused.

"I do," John admitted. "It makes them seem even more sinister, if that's possible. But you're avoiding my question."

"No I'm not. You didn't ask a question," Jessica pointed out. John thought and made a face; she was right. Jessica smiled and continued. "But, I do agree with you. I've had some time to think about all of this with you gone, and I'll one up you." John raised his eyebrow in anticipation. "I think Trip thinks the same thing."

"You know . . . no, that doesn't work," John said, shaking his head.

"No, out with it. Maybe if you say it, I'll catch something, or you will work something out," Jessica encouraged.

"I was supposed to be just a consultant on the whole undercover thing, but then it became me going undercover," John began. Jessica nodded, and John continued. "I always thought it was weird, but I keep forgetting it wasn't Kenneth that was president then. "

"That happened shortly after President Harrison was hurt in the skiing accident. Do you think maybe Harrison was in on it?" Jessica asked. John gave a low whistle.

"What would Harrison have to gain?" John asked. Jessica shrugged.

"I don't know," she admitted. "I just know that seems to be the point where both Trip and Jeremiah look the most uncomfortable when we talk about this case. Even when we met at the Moores before you got shot, they just seemed quite uncomfortable." Jessica gave a head shake and started to leave. She remembered something and turned around. "Did I tell you Jeff and Steve are no longer with the FBI?" John looked up, grinning. Jeff and Steve were two agents that got into the pocket of Archibald after they had been dressed down by Jessica and John for not doing their jobs very well.

"No, did they get busted when Archibald went to prison?" John asked.

"Archibald ratted them out when he 'got religion,'" Jessica said, using finger quotes. John snickered.

"Has he told anything useful yet?" he asked.

"Nope," Jessica replied. "A lot of little things like that. The warden thinks he's going to give up the mother-load any day. There's a preacher meeting with Archibald almost daily now, an Adam Johnson."

"I'm assuming he's been checked out thoroughly?" John asked. Jessica nodded. John looked down at the message in front of him. "Any idea when Ron took this?" he asked, holding up the phone number.

"I haven't seen it before, so I guess sometime today," Jessica replied.

"This is why I need a signal," John said to the note in complete seriousness. Jessica shook her head.

"You could ask Ron," Jessica suggested. John shook his head.

"I think Ron has gotten his first full dose of me and wasn't prepared for it," John said, studying the message. Jessica laughed. "Guess I better make the phone call." Jessica smiled and left the room. John picked up the phone to make a call that would change his life forever.

Chapter 10

John called the number left on the note that Ron had given him. There was no name, just a number and the words, "information on Nichols." John had no hope that this was anything other than a wild goose chase, but who else knew that he was looking into Kenneth Nichols? That was what was bothering John. The number wasn't one he recognized. He pushed those thoughts to the side as he heard a click on the other line. There was no voice, but he did hear breathing.

"Hello?" John said, confused. There was a pause, and then, there was a voice, one that nearly dropped him to his knees.

"I didn't think you'd call," the voice said softly. John's knees buckled.

"Sam?" he whispered forcefully. Jessica looked up from her desk at that moment, saw John, leapt up, and rushed into his office. She grabbed him before he fell to the floor. It was one thing to have seen what he thought might or might not have been the ghost of Sam, but to hear her voice... it was more than he could take. Jessica helped John into a chair and took the receiver from his hand. She looked at it like it was a snake.

"Who is this?" she hissed into the phone, not daring to wonder what or who would have caused a reaction like that from John.

"Put him on," the voice said forcefully, but softly. Jessica jerked back and looked at the phone with sheer confusion; she put her ear back to the receiver. "Sam?"

"No," the voice on the other end answered. Jessica closed her eyes and collected herself. She looked at John as she spoke.

"Amanda?" Jessica asked.

"I take it you both think I sound like my mother, Samantha?" Amanda said, putting extra emphasis on Samantha. Her father hated the use of the nickname Sam.

He said it destroyed the beauty and class of her name. "I need to talk to him." Jessica nodded, realizing in the back of her head that Amanda couldn't see what she was doing. She looked at John who had somewhat recovered. He cleared his throat and set his jaw.

"I can handle this," he said. Jessica gave him a concerned look. John reached out his hand to take the receiver. Hesitantly, Jessica handed it to him. John gave her the most reassuring smile he could muster.

"I apologize," John said into the receiver. "You do sound like your mother, and it caught me off guard. I never noticed it before when we had our earlier chats."

"Too busy checking me out?" Amanda asked. John was surprised and a little flustered. He was trying to think of what to say when he heard a chuckle on the other end of the phone. "You are way too serious," she chided. John gave a rueful smile and thought she was her mother's daughter. "I've called because I believe my life may be in danger." She paused. At this point she hadn't betrayed him, but she knew if she went any further, then there would be no holding back.

"Excuse me?" John asked. Amanda thought for just a second about hanging up, but she knew that if she did, she would be in this alone. "I'm sorry, you surprised me," John said. "Who would want to hurt you?"

"My father," she answered defiantly. She was going to do this, and she was going to do this the way her mother would have. "I think Kenneth Nichols, former President of the United States of America, is going to kill me." John was silent from shock. "John, are you there?" John looked up at Jessica, fire burning in his eyes. Amanda wasn't his daughter, but she was Sam's and he knew he owed Sam.

"I am," John answered. Jessica couldn't hear but one side of the conversation, but she was concerned. "Do you have any proof?" What John heard next changed his life forever.

"I have proof. I have a book that I believe has access codes and passwords and names that would bring down his empire," Amanda said. "I think I believe you..." Amanda paused to gather herself. "I think he took advantage of my mother and had her killed."

Amanda Nichols
Two Hours Earlier

Chapter 11

Amanda stared at all the newspaper clippings and articles in front of her that she had collected from various places over the past several days. She had copies of classified documents she shouldn't have but was given because of who she was. Everything she read was troubling. She knew there was only one of two answers. The first was all of the information in front of her was a lie, an out and out bald-faced lie. The other option, the one giving her the start of an ulcer, was that her father had lied to her. She tore her gaze away from papers in front of her and stared out the window at the skyline.

Amanda had gone to the cemetery where her mother was buried and looked for her gravestone and, to her chagrin, had found it. It said her name was Amanda Moore, instead of Amanda Nichols, but if what her mother's husband had told her was true, then that would have been consistent with his story.

Amanda was troubled. Her mother's husband, John, had told her that her father was the one that had kept Amanda from her mother, not him. Rage ran through Amanda. She glanced at the case she kept. Her father had given it to her in case something had ever gone wrong. She was to give it to either of his two associates, but she was never to look in it for any reason. Her entire life she had no reason to not believe her father, until now.

She looked back over the mountain of evidence that showed her mother's husband had told her the truth and that her father had lied. Amanda thought how her father had told her so many times that she could never believe the words of others and that people constantly tried to tear him down. She turned again and looked at the case. Her eyes narrowed, and she knew this had to end. She got up, opened the case, and looked inside at the contents. There were papers, which looked like bank accounts, that had insane amounts of money in them. She saw several thumb drives, picked one up, and put it in a laptop. She tried to open it, but numbers just ran across her screen. She figured it was encrypted. She took the thumb drive out and went back to the documents. She studied the papers again and was positive they were bank accounts. She opened a website to one of the banks and entered the account number. Amanda thought about it for a second and put her name and birthday in as the password, and the account opened. She dug through more papers and found some names. The names were troubling. She had heard them before and never in a positive light.

She bowed her head and wondered what her father was doing associating with mob bosses, known felons, and other people of ill repute. She looked at her phone and knew of only one way to find out.

Chapter 12

Amanda picked up the phone and called her father. The phone rang several times before it was answered.

"Amanda," said the panicked voice on the other end. "Is something wrong?"

"I'm okay, Dad," Amanda said. "But, something is wrong."

"What is it? I'm a little pressed for time," Kenneth said, sounding a little annoyed.

"It's the things you've told me, Father," Amanda said, bracing for the explosion. "A lot of things don't add up with newspaper clippings, reports, and other information I have." There was dead silence for a moment.

"Are you checking up on me?" Kenneth hissed through the receiver. "Are you checking up on me? The man who saved you when your mother abandoned you?"

"That's just it. My mother thought I was dead," Amanda answered.

"Who told you those lies?" Kenneth demanded. Amanda hesitated. "Was it John Fowler? Answer me, girl! It was John Fowler, wasn't it?"

"It's not just that," Amanda answered hurriedly. "I saw my gravestone. They all thought I was dead."

"You believe them over me?" Kenneth sneered.

"Daddy, why are you being like this?" Amanda asked, scared of the answer.

"Because you're just like her," Kenneth spat.

"Like who?" she asked, bracing herself for the tirade she knew was coming.

"Your mother!" Kenneth shouted. "I do everything for you, and you take the word of him over me? Do you know who I am? Well? DO YOU?"

"You're my father," Amanda whispered. Amanda heard an evil chuckle on the other end.

"I'm the last person you want to cross," Kenneth said quietly. "I'm the person who will sacrifice everything to get what I want. Do you understand that?" Amanda lowered her head. John had told her the truth. Her father had taken her from her mother. Rage boiled through Amanda. She looked over at the case on the floor and decided it was time that he learned exactly who she was.

"That's unfortunate," Amanda said in a low voice, dripping with hate and malice. Kenneth, for one of the few times in his life, was surprised by Amanda's reaction. He had feared this day would come, but he thought it would be later. Amanda always did whatever he wanted. She was a good little girl that always pleased her father, and now, it sounded as though she was more like him than he thought. "You might keep in mind that I am the person with your contingency plan." Kenneth winced. He had never thought Amanda would use the case against him. Kenneth checked his watch. It was going to be time for him to take care of his father in a few hours, and he couldn't get sidetracked with her now.

"Amanda," he began, keeping his voice under control. "Don't do anything hasty."

"Like turning over the contents of this case to the FBI if you don't tell me what happened to my mother?" she asked, venom in her voice. Kenneth squeezed his eyes shut. He opened them and decided he needed to deal with this quickly.

"I didn't kill your mother. You've seen the man arrested for it," Kenneth said.

"It wasn't your idea?" Amanda asked.

"No," Kenneth replied, hoping she would calm down.

"Why didn't my mother know I was alive?" she asked. "Why did she think I was dead?" Kenneth cursed to himself. There was no way to get out of this. "Do you really want me to call the FBI?"

"I had my father tell her you were dead!" Kenneth screamed into the phone. "I took advantage of your mother and had to hide it! Are you happy?" Kenneth was breathing hard. There was silence on the other line. "You are only one of four people to know that! Are you happy?" Still silence. Kenneth was furious, and he was losing control. "You, me, your grandfather, and my friend."

"Is that why Granddad is in jail?" she asked quietly. There was no answer from Kenneth. "Answer me!" she screamed.

"Yes," Kenneth sneered. "But I'm about to go take care of that, and then, you and I are going to have a little talk, young lady." Kenneth ended the call. Amanda stared at the phone. What was she going to do?

Chapter 13

Amanda decided there was only one person that could help her, and that was John. She called his office, but he wasn't there. She calmly left a message and waited. It was a few hours before he called back. There was a bit of confusion between the two of them and his new wife, Jessica. After she told him that her father was going to kill her, John pushed past the confusion and got down to business.

"What do you need me to do?" John asked. He knew he had to handle this carefully for multiple reasons. If he pressed her to come in, Amanda could easily revert back to the years of what John thought of as programming. Kenneth had taught her to hate him, Sam, and Jessica. If she was making this phone call because she seriously thought she was in trouble and not setting John up, then she and Kenneth must have had some type of falling out.

"I don't know," Amanda answered truthfully. "This is hard for me to wrap my mind around. For years…" she paused. John held his breath. He knew at some point in time he had to say something, but he wasn't good at this sort of thing. He closed his eyes and silently wished Sam was here to help him. He felt hands on his shoulder, opened his eyes, and jerked his head around, expecting to see Sam. It was Jessica, but in her eyes, he saw understanding and encouragement. John set his jaw and nodded.

Looking at Jessica the entire time he spoke, "We'll do this however you want to do it." Jessica smiled and nodded.

"I don't know what to do," Amanda said.

"Do you want me to alert the secret service to keep a close eye on him?" John asked. Amanda chuckled.

"You've not figured everything out yet," Amanda replied. John didn't understand what that meant. Amanda continued on. "Don't bother trying to call this number again. I'm going to get rid of it. If I decide to come in, I'll let you know." John hated to let her go, but there was something he wanted to do, and to do it right, he needed her permission.

"There are two other people who really should know of your existence," John said quietly. Jessica gave John a look. Worry covered her face, and John could tell she didn't agree with his decision, but it was done, and all she could do was wait and see. There was a silence on the other end for a few seconds.

"You're talking about the Moores," Amanda said.

"Yes," John replied, not trusting himself to say anything more.

"I'm not coming to a backyard reunion picnic," she said.

"Well, that won't be a problem since they don't do those," John replied, a grin growing on his face. "Now they might want to have a formal sit down dinner or something. I always get the forks confused at those things." Amanda chuckled. John glanced at Jessica. She was holding her hands, her fingers interlocked, in front on her face. John was a little puzzled. He saw so many emotions on her face and tears in her eyes.

"I would have assumed my mother would have taught you," Amanda said, causing John to pull his gaze from Jessica.

"Oh, she tried," John replied. "But, some might say I'm hopeless."

"What did she see in you?" Amanda asked, her tone light.

"I've been asking myself that for years," John replied honestly. Amanda chuckled.

"You're a conundrum, John Fowler," she said and disconnected the call. She disassembled the phone, gathered her things, and left the room of the cheap hotel.

On the other end of the phone call, John stared at the receiver for a minute.

"She's just like her," John said to the handset.

"And, everyone knows you beat the odds when you won Sam," Jessica said with a grin on her face. John turned to her. "Who says you can't do it again?" John had no answer for that, but he didn't think he had the faith that Jessica did.

Chapter 14

Dwayne looked around the nightclub at all the women and wondered who he was going to take home tonight. It was then he spotted her. She was pretty and blond, exactly the way he liked them. That's the way his mother looked before she had turned to pills, booze, and any man who would have her.

Dwayne felt the memories rushing back of her boyfriend beating on Dwayne as his doped-up mother just watched. He smiled as he thought about how she finally shot her boyfriend after he had beaten her after he got tired of beating on Dwayne. He remembered how his mother lied to him that they were never going to be hurt again. Dwayne remembered finding a knife in her boyfriend's pocket and stabbing her in heart after she passed out from the drugs and alcohol. Dwayne was a smart kid; he pulled the knife out of his mother carefully, so no trace evidence could get on him. He had read about trace evidence in one of his mystery books. Dwayne had wiped the handle clean and placed the knife into his mother's boyfriend's hand. After that, he called the police, crying. There wasn't much of an investigation.

Dwayne thought his life would get better being away from his mother, but that wasn't the case as he bounced from foster home to foster home. It was only after he was taken in by Paul that his life finally got better. Paul was a bladesmith. Dwayne watched Paul and eventually learned from him how to make his own knives, although he rarely did. On his eighteenth birthday, Paul told Dwayne he would make him anything he wanted. Dwayne asked for fifty identical knives. When Paul asked him why, Dwayne responded, "I lost count of how many boyfriends my mom had at 50, and I want something to always remind me that even though something can be used for pain, it doesn't have to be. I want something to show me that life doesn't have to be full of hurt."

Paul simply nodded and began to work on the knives. He finished them shortly and presented them to Dwayne. He told Dwayne that he had made each one identical. Dwayne thanked him, and for the first time in his life, he thought that life was going to be alright. The next morning when he woke, Paul was still in bed which was unusual for him. Dwayne went to check on him, but Paul was dead. It appeared to Dwayne that it was natural causes, but Dwayne was not a doctor. Dwayne sat there for several minutes, not sure what to do. He finally got up, put his knife set in his car, came back inside, and called the police. After the police and coroner took care of Paul's body, Dwayne packed his things and left. As he drove, he thought of his mother and the mess she had left him in. He stopped at a gas station several hours after he had started driving. After he filled up, he noticed the girl behind the cash register resembled his mother. Dwayne felt the anger and pain well up inside of him. A few hours later, after the girl's shift ended, her body was found with a knife sticking out of her heart and no other clues. Dwayne and his 49 remaining knives were already another state away, feeling like he had finally released all the rage he had ever possessed.

Chapter 15

Dwayne watched the pretty blond at the bar. She turned and saw him staring at her. Dwayne knew he was busted, but he didn't care. He wanted her. She smiled at him, and Dwayne knew he was going to get rid of some pent-up rage tonight. He walked over to her.

"Hello, beautiful," he said. "I'm Dwayne." The blonde stuck her hand out.

"I'm Liz," she said, giving his hair a hard look. "Tell me. I can't really tell in these lights. Is your hair brown?"

"Yeah, dark brown," Dwayne responded, wondering what kind of weirdo she was. "Is there some reason you want to know?"

"It reminds me of someone," she responded, with a smile on her lips.

"Not someone bad, I hope." Dwayne hated getting shot down because of something some other jerk had done. It was a shame Dwayne had to kill her. There was something about her. She leaned in close to whisper in his ear.

"It makes me have crazy thoughts," she replied, just loud enough to be heard over the music. She placed her hand on his leg and slowly started dragging it up his thigh. "Wanna get out of here?" Dwayne turned so he could see her face and smiled.

"I have a hotel room a few blocks from here," he replied, wondering if she had any idea how crazy things were about to get. She hopped off the bar stool, and Dwayne followed her. They walked down the street in silence; both intent on their destination. Dwayne had met some wild women in his time, but never one this forward. They reached the hotel, and Liz looked around.

"Sorry, I'm on a budget," Dwayne said as way of an excuse for the condition of the establishment. Dwayne wanted to make sure there were no cameras, and no one would bother him.

"It's fine," Liz said with a smirk on her face. "It looks like we can do whatever we want to, and no one will bother us." Dwayne shook his head, led her up the stairs, and let them in his room.

"Do you have a ladies room I could use, to get ready?" she asked. Dwayne pointed to it and went to his bag. He picked out his blade to get ready. He stood to the left of the door, waiting for her to exit. She stepped out and quickly turned to right where the bed and chair were. Dwayne stepped behind her, brought his left arm quickly under her neck, and was ready to use his right hand to drive the knife through her heart. That's when he noticed the revolver in her hand. She had put her hand through a roll of duct tape and the roll hung from her left wrist. Stunned by what he saw, Dwayne let her go. Liz turned to face him and saw the knife. They both looked at each other, in shock. They both dropped their weapons and rushed into each other's arms.

Dr. Brian Nichols
Present, Secure Location

Chapter 16

Dr. Nichols watched the lawyers leave the room and was once again by himself - if you didn't count all the marshals that were watching him and the house. Brian didn't know how much more of this he could take. His nerves were beginning to fray. He was the only thing standing between Archibald Staples being a free man and spending his life in prison. Brian had turned state's evidence against Archibald, but there was not enough to hold Archibald without Brian's testimony. Brian sat back and thought about how he got to where he was today. It had all started with his son, Kenneth. At an early age, Brian worried about his son and for good reason. Kenneth had something very wrong with him. He believed that he could do anything he wanted with no regard to others. During his teenage years, he began to spend a lot of time with Archibald. Brian wondered if he hadn't been working so much then if he could have done something about it.

What Brian didn't realize was Kenneth's infatuation with Samantha Moore. When Kenneth told Brian what happened, and then, Kenneth told Brain how to fix it, Brian should have gone to the police right then. Kenneth might have served time in prison, but it would have been better than what had occurred. For whatever reason, be it Kenneth's charm or Brian's fear of Kenneth, Brian went along with Kenneth's plan, and it worked.

Brian and Kenneth hid the baby that was produced by Kenneth's deed. No one but the two of them and Archibald knew what had happened. Brian always wondered if the Moores suspected. After that, Brian found himself going along with all of Archibald's and Kenneth's schemes. At some point - Brian wasn't sure when - Brian was helping Archibald and Kenneth build their empire by faking baby deaths and selling them on the black market. Brian wasn't sure what else the other two were involved in. He suspected they were selling illegal aliens into slavery, but he cast a blind eye to it as the money began to pour in.

At some point, Kenneth and Archibald found another partner, a low life mobster named Duck, and then, the money really seemed to come rolling in. Somehow, Duck rose to the top of the Mafia, Kenneth became Vice-President and then President of the United States, and Archibald Staples became one of the most powerful men in industry. It was all going so well until it wasn't. First Kenneth had to resign from the presidency, and then Brian was caught and was forced to turn over evidence on Archibald. Brian wondered how long until he was dead. It was inevitable now. Being the father of a former president meant nothing to men like Duck and Archibald, and Brian knew it. The only thing Brian hoped was to keep his son safe, but deep down, Brian knew Kenneth was lost years ago.

Chapter 17

Outside the house, Kenneth walked up to the two US Marshals that were parked in front of the safe house. They instantly recognized him.

"Mr. President," one of the Marshalls said as a way of greeting. Kenneth smiled.

"Former," Kenneth answered with a wry grin on his face. The marshal appeared embarrassed, but Kenneth just smiled at the marshal. "It's not your fault I married a crazy lady," Kenneth joked.

"I'm sorry about your loss, sir," the other marshal said. Kenneth just simply nodded.

"I hate to ask this guys. I know I'm not supposed to know who you are guarding, but it's pretty obvious I do," Kenneth said. The two marshals grinned. "Do you think I could go inside and just talk to my dad for a minute?"

The two marshals exchanged glances. The first one that Kenneth talked to radioed to the marshals that were inside and told them that the former president was coming inside to see his dad. Someone started to argue, but apparently the marshal Kenneth had first spoken to had rank, and the discussion quickly ended.

"Thank you, guys," Kenneth said and started toward the door. Kenneth went up to the door, knocked, and was allowed inside. The marshal inside let the former president in and then stepped outside. Kenneth made his way through the house and found his father in the back room.

"Hi, Dad," Kenneth said. Dr. Brian Nichols went pale when he heard the words. He knew that voice anywhere.

"What are you doing here?" Dr. Nichols asked quietly. Kenneth reached into his coat, pulled out a gun, and then began screwing a silencer onto it.

"Doing what I told you I'd do if you messed things up," Kenneth answered. Dr. Nichols quietly began to pray.

John Fowler
New York FBI Office

Chapter 18

John had never been to the Watergate Apartments before, and it took him a bit to remember that they were in Washington, D.C. He had decided he had better clear everything with Trip. John knocked on Trip's door with Jessica right behind him. Trip looked up and saw the two of them.

"Why am I worried?" Trip asked.

"Pressure of the job?" John asked.

"Panic attacks?" Jessica offered.

"Seen too many bad cop movies?" John added.

"Are you two done?" Trip asked, not wanting them to know he was enjoying the banter. John turned to Jessica who thought and nodded. John turned back to Trip and nodded for him to go on.

"I thought better of you Agent Hammerstein," Trip said, holding back the grin. "You've let him rub off on you." John smiled, proudly. Jessica stomped his foot, never taking her eyes off Trip. Trip roared with laughter. Jessica joined in, while John hopped on one leg. Trip took his glasses off and wiped the tears from his eyes from laughing. "What are you two up to?"

"The vice-president wants to meet John in D.C., and we feel we need to tell the Moores the existence of Amanda," Jessica said. John sat down while Jessica was talking, took off his shoe, and began to examine his foot. Jessica looked at him, sighed in mock exasperation, and took the seat beside him.

"We thought it might be best if we talked to the Moores now that we know of her existence," John said, all while flexing his toes. "Maybe now that they know she is alive, they'll allow themselves to think about things." Trip furrowed his eyebrows thinking about what John said.

"Are you saying they might have been covering something up?" Trip asked.

"Not exactly," John replied, putting his shoe back on. Jessica was shaking her head at the train wreck she called her husband. "They've always thought Amanda was dead and didn't dwell on what happened back then. Now that they know different, maybe they'll think more about that day." Trip thought about it and decided that wasn't a bad idea.

"Both of you going?" Trip asked.

"I'm going with John but not the meeting with the vice-president," Jessica answered.

"Sounds good," Trip said, going back to his files. "See you in a few days." Jessica and John exited the room, leaving Trip by himself. Trip closed the files and sat back in thought. After everything John and Jessica had been through, he wondered what they would do, if what Trip suspected had happened all those years ago were true.

Chapter 19

Jessica and John headed to the car for their road trip. They stopped by their apartment and grabbed the bag each of them kept ready for quick trips like this one. Jessica drove, which was the norm. John didn't know when that started happening. Well, that was a lie. Jessica started driving on their first case and rarely gave up the wheel to John. It wasn't a sexist thing with John; he just liked to drive every now and then. The drive would take most people between three and a half and four hours. John figured they would get there in under three. Jessica was known to have somewhat of a lead foot.

"Worried?" Jessica asked, breaking the silence. She glanced over to see John shrug his shoulders.

"I think the Cats could use some more outside shooting, but the coach seems to know what he's doing," John replied. Jessica rolled her eyes, and a grin began to form on John's face. "Don't hit me," he said, raising his hands in defense. John got serious. "How would you react if you thought your granddaughter had been dead for over twenty years, and now, you find out that she had been hidden from you?" Jessica shook her head; she had no answer for that.

"You have a plan, right?" she asked. Jessica thought John had a plan, but he had yet to share it, and those were the ones she always feared. John shrugged. "Come on. Tell me." John shook his head. There was a look on his face that Jessica had rarely seen, and that was the look of defeat.

"Sam deserved to know her," he said softly. Jessica took a calming breath. There it was, the reaction she had been waiting for. When all this started with Amanda, Jessica's biggest worry was John's reaction. For a few weeks, he had been handling it well, but John didn't do emotions well. John didn't do emotions at all. Things were black and white in John's eyes, and this was neither.

On one hand, it was amazing Amanda was alive, but on the flip side, she was raised by her father, and it seemed her prime mission was to kill John. Sam had wanted kids her entire life, and that made her never meeting Amanda a tragedy, but on the other hand, Jessica knew her friend would only want the best for Amanda and would expect Jessica to do all she could for Amanda.

"You've handled this very well," Jessica said, trying to get John to keep talking about things so that he wouldn't shut down on her. John turned to her and gave a sad smile.

"I'm just doing what Sam would want," he responded, and with that, he was quiet. Jessica didn't know what to say, and the two sat in silence for the remainder of the ride. A few hours later, Jessica pulled in front of the Watergate Apartments.

"You coming?" John asked. Jessica shook her head. "I'm sorry I've been moody."

"What we're dealing with isn't in most of those marriage books," Jessica said with a smile on her face.

"I'm not writing one," John said, completely serious. Jessica laughed and waved him off. John got out of the car and entered the complex. He was met by members of the Secret Service and was escorted to an apartment. One of the Secret Service agents knocked on the door, and it opened. John was led inside. Jeremiah was there waiting for him with a woman that looked very familiar to John.

"I'm here, Jeremiah," John said. "What's so important that you couldn't tell me over the phone?"

"Ma'boy," Jeremiah began. "This is one of those things I can only show you, not tell you." With that, he led John into another room. As John passed by the woman in the room, he realized it was the former first lady. John went through the door that Jeremiah opened and was very surprised by who he saw on the other side.

Chapter 20

"John, I'd like you to meet President Harrison," Jeremiah said. John noted that Jeremiah did not say former when he introduced the president. John reached out and shook the former president's hand.

"Good to meet you, son," he said. "Senator Cosby here has said so many nice things about you." John was a little confused but saw the look on Jeremiah's face and just went with it. "Jeremiah here is telling me that he thinks this new taskforce you've started is going to lead to some big things." The former president leaned in close. "Don't tell anyone, but I think we could use you to bring down organized crime. There are those around me that think you are the perfect man for the job." John didn't know what to say or do. His mind was spinning. If he didn't know better, President Harrison didn't remember meeting him and discussing how they were going to bring down the mob. Jeremiah made the save.

"Well, Mr. President, we don't want to take any more of your time. John's got lots to do," Jeremiah said. The former president shook John's hand again, and John and Jeremiah left the room. When they shut the door behind them, John turned to Susan.

"What just happened?" he asked, completely confused. "I saw a newspaper in the room, and it was dated years ago. There are dated pictures are on the wall, and the former president had no idea we had ever met. What is going on?" Susan gave Jeremiah a look.

"You did say he would catch on quick," Susan said to Jeremiah. Jeremiah just smiled. Susan turned to John. "I'm about to let you in on one of the biggest political secrets in this country's history, John. But first you need some backstory to understand everything." John nodded, curious to know where this was going to go.

"Right after the reelection, the president had an accident," Susan said. John thought back and remembered the skiing accident that had hurt the president and even had his then Vice-President Kenneth Nichols in charge of the country for a few days. John nodded, and Susan continued. "What we told the nation was the president was physically injured, but what we never told them was that he had amnesia, and not just any amnesia. He has Anterograde Amnesia." John just looked at Susan, not sure what that meant. Susan thought for a second and continued. "There was a comedy movie about a girl who suffered from it," Susan began.

"John doesn't watch a whole lot of pictures, Susan," Jeremiah interjected. Susan nodded.

"He can't make new memories," Susan said, waiting for the questions that she was used to once she told someone this news.

Dr. Brian Nichols
Secure Location

Chapter 21

"Dad," Kenneth began, the pistol pointed at Brian.
"I warned you what would happen if you failed at your job.
We all warned you to not get involved with the babies.
Why did you need the money? You were set!" Brian
watched his son slowly begin to lose his temper. Brian
knew he had only minutes left in his life.

"I'm sorry, son," Brian said softly, his head down,
dejected. "I got greedy." Kenneth nodded.

"I'm proud of you, Dad," Kenneth said. Surprised,
Brian, looked at his son. "You told the truth, and you're
going to take your comeuppance like a man. It will be a
good final memory of you."

"They'll find out you killed me," Brian said.
Kenneth just smiled, and Brian's heart sank.

"They'll never find a trace of me," Kenneth said.
"Besides, who are they going to compare anything they
find to, and who's going to believe I killed my father?"

Brian shut his eyes. His son was crazy, and he was
going to die. There was only one thing left.

"Take care of her," Brian said softly, his eyes still
shut. The feeling in the room changed. Brian opened his
eyes, and he could see the hatred and seething on
Kenneth's face.

"She turned on me, Father," Kenneth said. "She's
going to pay."

"Kenneth, she's your daughter," Brian replied.
Kenneth raised the gun quickly and fired two bullets in
succession into Brian's head. Brian fell off the bed and hit
the ground, dead.

"And, you were my father," Kenneth said,
unscrewing the silencer. He walked out of the room and
then out of the house. He waved at the marshals. "You

might give him a minute," Kenneth shouted to the men. "He gets kind of emotional after our meetings." The men nodded, and Kenneth continued on, wondering if the Marshals would be fired after they accused him of killing his father. All of his secret service agents would say that he was at his house. Kenneth smiled. It was good to be him. Now, it was time to deal with his backstabbing daughter. He would hate to lose her, but sometimes, you had to punish your children.

John Fowler
Watergate Apartments

Chapter 22

John's mind was moving quickly, processing what Susan had just told him. The former president didn't know anything that had happened since the accident. Everything he did, he forgot. John thought back to when he and the president had initially met to discuss the mob idea. Something bothered him. He looked at Jeremiah who was watching John's face intently.

"Go with it, son," he said softly. John nodded and closed his eyes. Jessica had taught him this trick when he had first saw Amanda. At first, he had thought she was Sam, but when he mentally compared the two, it was obvious they were different. John began to access the memories. He compared heights. They were close. The change in age could account for the slight differences. The same could be said with facial differences and weight, but there was something. There was something that wasn't right. John's eyes popped open, and he looked at Jeremiah. Tears were in Jeremiah's eyes, and John didn't need his abilities to read what was on Jeremiah's face. The secret. John's mind was screaming. It was the only possible answer. The secret Jeremiah carried. It wasn't possible, but it was the only thing that made sense. Horror spread across John's face. Jeremiah couldn't speak; he only nodded. John turned to Susan. The look on her face told John all he needed to know.

"Jeremiah said that you were the best. He wasn't kidding," she said simply.

John couldn't believe what he was hearing, seeing, and even sensing.

"When you have eliminated the impossible, whatever remains, however improbable, must be the truth,"

Jeremiah quoted. John turned to him, not trusting himself to speak. Jeremiah shook his head. "Spit it out, boy!"

"The man I met that sent me undercover," John began, Jeremiah nodding, trying to help the words out of John. "That wasn't the president." The last words weren't a question.

"And, now, you know my darkest secret," Jeremiah said softly. John turned to Susan who was slowly nodding.

"The question is, what are you going to do about it?" she asked.

Kenneth Nichols
Secure Location

Chapter 23

Kenneth whistled tunelessly as he returned to his residence. It was surprising how little it had cost to have his father's secure location to be positioned so close to his residence. He snuck in through the tunnel he had built in the house beside his. None of his secret service men knew of it. All they knew was that Kenneth Nichols was safe and sound inside his personal residence. They knew that there was a young blond girl they were supposed to let in anytime she wanted, but none of them asked why. Kenneth knew he needed to have that privilege revoked from his daughter. She should hope that was the only thing he took from her. Kenneth shook the thoughts from his mind.

He came up the basement stairs, looked around, and headed to the master bedroom. He waited a few minutes, and the man he was waiting for walked in. The man disrobed, and then, Kenneth did. They switched clothes without saying a word. Kenneth started to leave the room.

"Should I stay nearby?" the man asked. Kenneth stopped and turned, looking at a mirror reflection of himself.

"No, you need to get out of town for a bit, and stay low," Kenneth said. "Things might get ugly for a little while." The man nodded, and Kenneth started to leave the room.

"You killed him, didn't you?" asked the man that looked like Kenneth. Kenneth smiled, stopped, and turned.

"My father killed himself when he testified, and he knew it," Kenneth replied. "Is that a problem, Rich?" Rich shook his head.

"No problem," he replied. "I just wanted to know what I might be accused of."

"You're not going to be accused of anything because if you're caught, you know what happens," Kenneth replied.

"Is that a threat?" Rich asked.

"No, it's a promise that I'll kill you and every member of your family if you ever say a word," Kenneth replied. Rich burst out laughing, and Kenneth smiled.

"If you need me, call me," Rich said, shaking the hand of his friend and partner in crime. With that, Rich left the room through the door in which Kenneth had initially entered. Kenneth stood for a minute after Rich left, and thought about his daughter. There was only one thing he knew to do. He decided he would sleep on what he was thinking about doing, and if he still felt the same way in the morning, he would arrange a meeting. He felt peace with that decision. He needed to act normally now, so he went into the living room to watch the news. Kenneth was curious to see who had died that day.

Chapter 24

John was shaking his head in disbelief. He couldn't believe what Jeremiah and Susan were saying.

"This is impossible," he said.

"Impossible, no," Jeremiah answered. "Improbable, yes." John looked at Jeremiah, not believing what he was hearing.

"How?" John asked softly.

"There were a couple of actors," Susan answered. John turned toward her. "We didn't know how bad the damage was to the president at the time. These two actors already resembled the president and vice-president." She paused a second and glanced at John, shame covering her face. "You have to understand that we weren't trying to trick anyone by doing something underhanded. We had no idea of the extent of the President's injuries." Tears were in Susan's eyes. John wondered how many people she had actually told this story to. Relief seemed to cover her face as she talked. She sniffed, regained her composure, and continued.

"Anyway, everyone knew the president had an accident, so the actor had a little plastic surgery and appeared with bandages," Susan said, glancing at the shut door that held her husband behind it.

"So, the man the country saw wasn't actually the President, but the actor?" John asked, wondering what kind of fantasy story he had wandered into. Jeremiah nodded. Susan kept staring at the door, refusing to look John in the face. John rubbed his hand over his face, still stunned by what he was hearing, but not sure how Kenneth fit into this. And, then, it hit him. If John had shock on his face earlier, what covered his face now was something much more. He turned to Jeremiah. Jeremiah had tears in his eyes and could only nod slowly. John turned toward Susan who was quietly sobbing.

"We destroyed everything we fought for," Jeremiah said softly. John turned toward him.

"I'm going to need you to tell me exactly what happened," John said, fearing he already knew. Jeremiah nodded.

"It's my story, Jeremiah," Susan said, still looking at the door. She turned to John and drew herself up. "Jeremiah didn't know for a long, long time." John nodded. Susan gathered herself. For the first time since John had entered the apartments, Susan resembled the strong First Lady he had remembered. John nodded for her to go on.

"Once Kenneth saw what happened, he seized his opportunity," Susan began. "At first, he told us that he ran the show. The actor that was playing my husband did everything that Kenneth told him."

"Including putting me undercover?" John asked. Susan nodded.

"Before the accident, Kenneth had already been in my husband's ear about that, and after he was incapacitated, there was no stopping him," Susan answered. John blew out a breath. That was one question answered. He thought that would be the biggest one going into tonight, but after what he had learned and seen, he knew there was one more.

Chapter 25

"That's not the big secret though, is it?" John asked. Susan shook her head. John looked over at Jeremiah. Jeremiah looked broken. That was the only word John could find to describe him. John thought about all the years he had known Jeremiah, and John didn't believe he had ever seen Jeremiah this way.

"The second actor, Rich, I believe is his name. He looked very similar to Kenneth," Susan began. She paused, took a breath, and continued. "Kenneth made Rich have plastic surgery as well. John, there is virtually no way to now tell them apart. Rich has Kenneth's every mannerism down. Rich knows tone, inflection, dialect, everything. Rich had been paid handsomely for his services, and he treats it as his job - his only job. Kenneth has been known to disappear some times for days on end, and no one has noticed." Susan stopped. She was fighting back tears. John couldn't believe what he was hearing, but he could tell Jeremiah and Susan weren't lying. What was worse, John had been playing every meeting, TV appearance, and picture he knew of Kenneth through his mind. His senses confirmed that there were slight differences. There was nothing the average person would notice, and they could all be attributed to stress, age, and other factors, but there was no denying it in John's mind. Kenneth had an actor to play him when he wanted him to.

"To what end?" John asked, knots forming in his stomach from what he was afraid was the answer.

"We truly don't know, ma'boy," Jeremiah answered quietly. "I can't believe it's for anything good." Jeremiah looked John in the eye. "I'm sorry, John. This wasn't my secret to share. I'm sorry I had to hold this from you." John nodded and looked over at Susan.

"For now, I'm going to keep quiet," John said. Susan looked shocked, and Jeremiah started to object. John held up his hand. "All I have right now is your word, and while that's good enough for me, I need proof, and honestly, I need to know what he did when this Rich character was filling in for him." John paused and gave the two a sad smile. "Besides, I don't think there's any good that can come of me exposing this to the American people. They don't trust politicians as it is. As far as I'm concerned, you two have reported everything to the proper authorities, and now, I'm just running my case. I need to use this secrecy to my advantage. Kenneth doesn't know that I know. I need every advantage I can get to figure out what exactly he is doing."

"I don't trust him, son," Jeremiah said. John nodded.

"I don't either," John answered. "Before I got shot, there was something Chet traced back to the White House. Chet thought the hacker had given him a false lead. I think Chet actually tracked a phone out of the White House. I think Kenneth is in league with Duck and Archibald." John grinned and looked directly at Jeremiah. "And, I think you think the same thing." Jeremiah grinned, surprising John, and nodded.

"It's in your hands, John," Susan said. "You do with the information that you've been given today what you think is necessary." John nodded and put his hat on his head, preparing to leave.

"I'll keep you out of this if I can," he said to Susan. John turned to Jeremiah. "You, too. Good night." And with that, he left. Jeremiah turned to Susan.

"There's something else I need to speak with him about," Jeremiah said, kissing Susan on the cheek. He hurried out the door, leaving Susan with her thoughts. She began to think about how things would have been if she hadn't gone along with the plan. She shook her head and headed into her husband's room to see how he was.

Chapter 26

John stood out in the hall, not knowing what to make of what he had just learned. He was lost in his thoughts and jumped when the door he just left opened. Jeremiah walked out, saw John, and paused. John studied him and instantly knew that he was about to find out even more than he had imagined.

"You didn't do this," John said softly.

"I didn't stop it," Jeremiah replied just as softly. John shook his head.

"You didn't benefit from this," John said.

"I'm the Vice-President now," Jeremiah responded. John didn't know how to answer that. "Let me tell you something else you need to know. Bruce has figured it out."

John closed his eyes. He reached his hand back to touch the wall. He wanted to make contact with something so that he wouldn't fall over. He wasn't having an attack, but he was scared he might. When he opened his eyes, he saw the concern on Jeremiah's face.

"I'm okay," John said. "I just have some bad memories when it comes to him."

"Rightfully so, ma'boy, rightfully so," Jeremiah said, nodding sagely. "I won't let him control me, John. You have my word on that." A grin crossed John's face.

"I never thought he would be able to, Jeremiah," John answered. Jeremiah chuckled.

"I have been known to be a bit cantankerous when it comes to that boy," Jeremiah admitted ruefully. John chuckled for a moment. He turned serious.

"I think I need to tell the Moores about Amanda," John said. Jeremiah nodded.

"They need to know, and you need to be the one to tell them," he replied. Jeremiah straightened and sighed deeply. "I've made a mess out of things,"

"Jessica and I are on our way to talk to them," John said, studying Jeremiah.

"Surely you're not hoping they know something about this horrible business," Jeremiah said - not asked. John lowered his head and didn't say anything. He looked back at Jeremiah, expecting to see disappointment in his eyes. John studied Jeremiah, and what he saw was more pity than disappointment. "Who are you doing this for, ma'boy?" Jeremiah asked softly.

"I don't know," John admitted, shaking his head. "Jeremiah," John paused, not wanting to say the words that he had been feeling. John knew once he said them, it made them seem more real. "She's my last link to Sam," John admitted, his voice trembling. "I know I have Jessica, and it's time to move on, but I also know how much Sam wanted children and how badly I messed that up for her. Don't I owe her?" Jeremiah shook his head; a sad smile covered his face.

"Let me ask you an honest question, Son. Would you feel the same way if this was happening to someone else? Would you move heaven and earth to figure out what was going on if this wasn't your widow and her daughter? Would you do all of this for some other man if he was in this position?" John stood motionless for a second and then slowly shook his head.

"I don't think I would," John admitted. Jeremiah nodded, and patted John on the shoulder.

"At least your honest, ma'boy," Jeremiah said. He gripped John's shoulder. "Keep in mind there's other people whose emotions are involved here such as that lovely bride of yours and the Moores." John nodded. Jeremiah took his hand off John's shoulder, shook his hand, turned, and left. John headed outside to the car and got in. He was so wrapped up in what he had just experienced that he didn't even notice the look on Jessica's face. Jessica started the car and raced away. John grabbed ahold of the handle bar above the door.

"Who's dead?" John asked in jest.

"Our star witness against Archibald," Jessica answered. John whipped his head around toward Jessica, took one look at her, and knew it was true. John held on to the handle bar, praying he would make it to the crime scene in one piece.

Chapter 27

"I don't suppose they have a suspect?"

John's question hung in the air. Jessica glanced over at him, still driving furiously to get to the crime scene.

"Will you please keep your eyes on the road?" John begged, while pointing toward the road. "It's too bad Dr. Nichols wasn't already in WITSEC."

"Do you really think they could have kept him alive?" Jessica asked, taking a curve a little fast. John swore they went up on two wheels.

"They're the best," John said definitively.

"Good enough to stop Archibald, or the mob, or whoever is in this evil cabal of yours?" John really wished Jessica would stop talking to him as she drove to the crime scene. The way she was driving, he thought she needed all of her focus on one thing; getting them there alive.

"Jess," John began carefully. "Dr. Nichols is dead, and I would like to get there alive." Jessica rolled her eyes but slowed down.

"What is it with you and me driving fast?" she asked, irritated.

"Fast? I don't think most races are run at the speeds you drive at!" Jessica shot John a look and made a turn. Lights were flashing everywhere.

"We're here safe and sound," Jessica said. The tone she used sounded like someone trying to soothe a baby.

"Don't start," John said, not meaning to snap at her, but after learning what former President Harrison had pulled and now the death of Dr. Nichols, his nerves were shot. Jessica raised her eyebrows at him in warning. "I'm sorry," he quickly apologized. Jessica had opened the door but quickly closed it and turned toward John.

"What happened back there?" John searched her face. He knew the look in her eyes. She was about to go full interrogation on him, and John didn't want that.

"I want you to listen to me very carefully," John began. Jessica's eyes squinted, pondering what he was about to say, or more likely, pull. "I don't know if I can tell you. I don't know if I have permission to tell you." Jessica was confused.

"Jeremiah wouldn't let you tell me?" she asked, trying to get clarification. John shook his head.

"I don't know if Jeremiah is the person that can grant that permission," John said with a look of defeat on his face. Jessica studied him. "I'm supposed to be the one that reads people not you." John couldn't resist the little dig.

"Shush," she said, thinking. She moved very close to him, less than an inch separated their faces. "There are very few people that Jeremiah would think he owed them their trust." John nodded. Jessica's brow crinkled, thinking. "So, if Jeremiah doesn't think he has permission, it's a very short list, but a list of very powerful people." John nodded again. Jessica crunched the side of her lip, thinking. She nodded and started to back away and then quickly moved forward, making John jump back. "I'll let it go…. for now." She started to pull away again, feinted moving back toward John, laughed at John jumping backwards again, and got out of the car.

"I married her. Why?" he asked no one, out loud.

"I heard that!"

Chapter 28

John and Jessica headed toward the home that was surrounded by flashing lights, crime scene tape, and several official looking people. As John reached a group, he overhead arguing.

"I'm telling you it was his son," one of the marshals was saying to a man in a suit. John was pretty sure the marshal was talking to his boss.

"I just talked to Secret Service," the man in the suit replied. "He never left their sight. Did he come with any of them?" The marshal looked down at the ground, embarrassed. John was reading both men as they talked, and they were both telling what they believed to be the truth. John stopped to study the men and quickly came to his own conclusion about what had happened.

"What is it?" Jessica asked carefully.

"Nothing good if I'm right," John replied cryptically. John walked over to the two men who had been talking. He showed the badge, and the man in the suit nodded.

"I'm sorry, Agent Fowler," the man in the suit said. "We got fooled."

"I don't think so," John answered. "Are there any techs at the scene?" The man in the suit nodded.

"Yes, and they are going to run the DNA against EVERY database," the man in the suit replied. John understood what he was stressing.

"You don't think there will be a match," John said-not asked. The man in the suit shook his head. John held his hand out to shake the man's hand, and when he took it, John moved in close.

"Has your agent ever messed up like this before?" John asked softly where no one else could hear him. The man in the suit shook his head. "Then, consider the fact that he didn't this time either." The man in the suit gave John a strange look, but John was already heading into the house. The body of Dr. Nichols had already been moved from the house, and John and Jessica were allowed to walk the crime scene. John walked in, observed the entire room, shook his head, and left the room. Jessica went inside and stayed for a bit, observing, studying, and almost engulfing the scene. John noticed some important looking people talking in a corner, not quite arguing, but not far from it. John hoped they were fighting over who was going to take the case, but he was pretty sure they were trying to figure out who to blame. John pulled out his cell phone and called Trip.

"There's a marshal here saying that Kenneth came into the house earlier tonight," John said. Silence met him from the other end. "It looked like Dr. Nichols was executed." Still silence. "I had a meeting tonight with a former president and one of our mutual friends at the Watergate Apartments tonight." John was rewarded with a slight gasp on the other end. There was a pause on the line.

"You're smiling, aren't you?" Trip asked.

"No," John lied, smiling. He started scratching at a spot that had just popped on his arm.

"So, you think you know what happened?" Trip asked.

"I have an idea, but how am I ever going to prove it?" John asked.

"I think most of what you need is at the Watergate Apartments," Trip countered.

"How is that going to prove that Kenneth did this?" John asked. "It gives me means, but I still have got to prove it all. Besides, do you think a judge will give me a warrant based on that?"

"Nope," Trip replied casually.

"And, that's why you never acted on anything you knew," John said.

"I never knew for sure," Trip admitted. "I had suspicions, especially after they put you undercover and while you were incapacitated,"

"Gutshot?" John asked.

"And, while you were incapacitated," Trip continued, ignoring John. "Jeremiah and I had a talk about hypotheticals. You know more than I do at this point, but unless you have a smoking gun, all we have is a lot of smoke, but no fire."

"So you think prints are going to come back useless?" John asked.

"Yep," Trip answered. "Go get some rest, and take care of your business with the Moores. I suspect you didn't plan all of this on your first day back."

"Nope," John replied. "I was expecting to get enough to bust the remainder of the cabal." Trip laughed and disconnected. Jessica exited the crime scene room, and the two of them left the house, returned to their car, and wordlessly continued their trip to the Moores.

Chapter 29

Jessica and John entered the Moores home very somber. Both of them had the same question on their minds. How do you tell two people the grandchild they thought had been dead for over twenty years, is alive? Rosa, a witness to many of Archibald's crimes, but one John and Jessica were very cautious about using given Archibald's history of witnesses turning up dead, led them into the main living room. John looked around the home that could only be described as a mansion. He still couldn't believe some days that Sam had grown up here. Rosa left the two of them in the room and went to get Arthur and Madeline, Sam's parents. They entered the room, looking as regal as ever. Madeline paused when she saw John's face.

"I don't need your abilities to know something is wrong," she said to John. "What's troubling you two?"

"I just hate it when she beats around the bush," John said to Arthur.

"I've tried to talk to her about being more direct but can't get her to change," Arthur admitted, shrugging.

"Oh, look, they think they're funny," Madeline said to Jessica. Jessica smiled at Madeline.

"They're so cute at that age," Jessica added. "At least they're talking to each other instead of shouting and gesturing with their hands constantly." Both women smiled and turned to look at the two men. John turned to Arthur.

"I'm not good at this kinda thing, but I think we're beat," John said.

"We were beat before we began," Arthur replied. "Now, what is bothering you?" John looked at Jessica. She nodded for him to go on.

"Maybe you two should sit down," John said, gesturing toward the couch. Madeline and Arthur exchanged glances and sat on the couch. Jessica sat in a chair across from them. John remained standing, trying to figure out how to tell them the news. Jessica blew air up from her bottom lip, getting impatient.

"Oh, for crying out loud," Jessica muttered. She sat forward and looked directly at Madeline and Arthur. "Your granddaughter is alive." Madeline blinked several times. John didn't know whether to be irritated with Jessica or hug her for getting him off the hook from telling them. Arthur's eyes began to tear up.

"Samantha's daughter?" Arthur asked. Jessica nodded.

"Her name's Amanda," John added. Arthur looked at Madeline. Madeline just stared at John and Jessica.

"Is she okay?" Madeline managed to ask.

"Physically, yes," John said. He chose his words very carefully. "Her father raised her, so emotionally . . ." John trailed off, not sure how to finish the sentence. Madeline listened for a second, taking it all in. She then slapped Arthur on the shoulder.

"I told you we should have followed up more," she said calmly, but underneath, there was no question of the intensity. Arthur shook his head, tears starting to run down his face.

"Does she want anything to do with us?" Arthur asked.

"She told me it was okay to tell you she was alive," John replied. "She thinks she may be in trouble with her father. She has finally realized her father is not the man he has always told her he was."

"Can we do anything?" Arthur asked.

"Not that I know of," John replied, shaking his head. "There may come a day she needs someplace to hide or stay -"

"Anything, money, a place to stay… you tell me, she'll get it," Arthur said, cutting in. John nodded.

Madeline and Arthur remain seated, not sure what to say. John felt like he was intruding.

"Look, I feel like we're intruding," John said. "We'll tell you anything you want to know, but it looks as though you two need to talk. Is it okay if we stay here tonight?"

"Certainly," Madeline said, standing. Arthur got up, while Jessica walked over to hug both of them. Jessica started upstairs, and John followed behind her slowly. "Samantha would expect you to take care of her," Madeline said softly. John turned and smiled.

"You know I will," John replied. Arthur nodded, and Madeline returned John's smile. Jessica and John headed upstairs. As he reached the room they were staying in, John heard voices from downstairs.

"Think they're okay?" Jessica asked. John shrugged.

"I guess," John replied.

"Are you okay?"

"I have no idea," John replied honestly. He changed clothes and climbed in bed. Jessica was asleep in what seemed like seconds, while John lay awake wondering what Sam would do.

Chapter 30

The next morning, John was very quiet at breakfast. Jessica talked to Madeline and Arthur about Amanda and if they had any more thoughts about the case now that they knew she was alive. Madeline and Arthur told Jessica everything they could think of, but all of it was old news to John. During the talk, John got a text from Trip, telling him that Archibald was going to be released from prison since the person testifying against him was dead. After a few minutes, John excused himself and began to walk the house and eventually the grounds.

John wandered the grounds until he found the pond he was looking for and the tree that sat on the bank. He searched the tree until he found his and Sam's initials carved into the tree. John knew he was much too old to have carved those initials when he did, but it made Sam happy so he had. He stood by the pond and waited. He didn't know what he was waiting for, but for the first time, he felt it, before she spoke.

"Thought you couldn't talk to me anymore?" John said, opening his eyes and looking over the pond.

"I married this guy a while back, and it seems I've taken to his belief that if he didn't make the rules, then it was okay to break them," the voice answered behind him. John turned and saw Sam. Tears filled his eyes, and he shook his head.

"I swore I wasn't going to cry this time," John said, rebuking himself.

"It's okay," Sam answered with a grin on her face and crinkling her nose. "It lets me know you care." She paused for a second, and a smile broke across her face. "Congratulations, by the way."

"Oh," John said, not sure what to say. "Well, I waited for you-"

"Oh, for crying out loud!" Sam exclaimed. "I'm happy for you two. I mean, it wasn't like you killed me to be with her or anything." John couldn't help but laugh.

"John, who are you talking to?" Jessica's voice asked before she walked up. "Oh!" John turned toward Jessica.

"You can see her?" John asked. Jessica nodded.

"You can, too?" Jessica asked. Sam waved her arms.

"She is right here," Sam said. Jessica walked up to John but wasn't sure what to do. "You two," she said, exasperated. Sam looked deadly serious. "Look, you can have therapy over this later, but I need you to do something."

"Anything," Jessica said, quietly but forcefully.

"I need you to divorce him," Sam said. Jessica looked stunned. A smile grew across Sam's face. "You have no idea how long I've been wanting to do that." John's jaw dropped, realizing he'd been duped. "Seriously, you two have got to help Amanda. She's going to cross him, and when she does, he will try and kill her."

"I'll protect her," John said. "Whatever it takes." Jessica nodded. Sam smiled at them.

"I am happy for you two, and you know I mean that," Sam said. She turned and started to leave.

"Did you know she was alive?" John asked. Sam stopped but didn't turn around.

"Not until I was dead," Sam answered. "I always hoped and believed, but I didn't know. Do me a favor. Tell my mom its time. She'll know what it means."

John looked at Jessica in confusion. She looked at him, and they both realized neither was watching Sam. They turned back to where she had been, and she was gone.

"I'm not divorcing him!" Jessica yelled and stuck her tongue out at the air.

"I know," Sam's voice came back from nowhere and everywhere. John stood there and turned toward the pond, just staring at it.

"Are you okay?" Jessica asked. John nodded.

"At least I know what she wanted me to do," John answered. "Are you going to be okay with this?" Jessica nodded.

"Sam came back to ask you to watch out for her daughter. How can I not be?" Jessica answered. John nodded and turned back toward the pond. All he had to do was find Amanda and help her against one of the most evil men he had ever known. This should be a piece of cake, he thought.

John and Jessica headed back to the house. They prepared to leave, while John thought of a good way to bring up what Sam had told him.

"Madeline," John said, pulling her to the side. "If I told you that Sam had told me to tell you it's time, would you know what that means?" Madeline gave John a strange look.

"I have some idea," Madeline admitted. "But, how could Sam have told you that?" John looked at her, then down at the ground. He lifted his head, trying to figure out how to tell her without sounding crazy when he noticed Madeline had a knowing smile on her face. "You know, there are days when I'm on the grounds that I still think I catch a glimpse of her. Don't you worry, dear. I know what it means." John thought about pressing her on it but decided to let things go. As John and Jessica got on the road, something occurred to John.

"How do you feel about a side trip?" John asked, a grin growing on his face.

"Why?" Jessica asked.

"To irritate someone we both can't stand." John replied. Jessica smiled.

"Where to?" she asked as they headed down the road.

Archibald Staples
Prison

Chapter 31

Archibald was in a meeting with Brother AJ when Brother AJ's phone went off. Brother AJ checked the phone and smiled.

"It appears my friend a miracle has occurred," Brother AJ said to Archibald. "It appears the witness in the case against you has tragically been murdered."

"I wonder how his son is taking the news?" Archibald asked with a sly grin on his face.

"Since he's the one who texted me, I would say fairly well," Brother AJ replied. "Apparently, your lawyer is working on getting you released, and it should happen within the next few hours." Archibald smiled happily.

"I think it's time to begin moneymaker," Archibald said. Brother AJ simply nodded. Archibald knocked on the door for his guard. Archibald was led through the prison and was returned to his cell. Over the next few hours, he sat in quiet meditation just waiting to be released. The doors to his cell opened, where a guard led him back toward the front gate. He switched out of his prison uniform into his own clothes. He was returned his personal affects, and he headed toward the door. His lawyer was double checking everything to make sure his client left with everything he came in with. They left through the front door and headed toward the parking lot. Archibald was smiling. A bus with prisoners was parked on one end of the lot. As they approached the car, they noticed that all four tires were flat on the car. Archibald stared at the car in disbelief. The bus behind them started up and pulled away, Archibald and his lawyer never paid attention to it. They were both staring at the car.

"You just can't believe some people anymore. Can you, Jess?" The voice came from behind Archibald.

Archibald was seething. He turned and stared at John and Jessica who were both wearing sunglasses and leaning against the side of a car. John was wearing his hat and holding a pocket knife, blade out. He was looking it over. "I mean, who would slice the tires on the care that belonged to Archibald Staples and his lawyer."

"I'll have your badge for this, Fowler!" the lawyer screamed. John shrugged.

"My fingerprints are on the knife. I did pick it up off the ground, and I'm sure that the entire bus full of prisoners will tell you I slashed the tires," John admitted. "But, I'm going to bet none of the guards on that bus are going to collaborate with the inmates. In fact, all you have is a bus full of convicted felons." Archibald held a hand up to his lawyer to stop him from launching into another tirade.

"What do you want, John?" Archibald asked. John closed the knife, took his sunglasses off, and walked over to Archibald. John looked Archibald up and down.

"They say you found religion in jail, Archibald," John said quietly. "I think you're playing one of your little games, like normal."

"Only God and I know what happened," Archibald answered. John nodded, a self-satisfied smile crossing his face.

"That's good, Archibald," John answered. He leaned in close where only Archibald could hear him. "I know you had something to do with my wife's death. I'm going to get you, Duck, and your buddy Kenneth." Archibald's face faltered for just a split second, but that's all John needed. "I'm going to get each of you, Archibald."

"I'll kill you," Archibald spat, loud enough for Jessica and the lawyer to hear him.

Chapter 32

John smiled. He had hoped to get Archibald riled up, but this was working better than he could have hoped. John decided to press on.

"Better men than you have tried," John replied. "Bruce may be stone cold crazy, but at least he had the guts to actually try to kill me, than to send someone after me." Archibald made a noise that sounded like a growl and looked like he was about to pounce John. The lawyer ran up and began to pull Archibald away. John turned to the lawyer. "Seems you and your client have no way home. Can we offer you a lift?" Archibald was seething.

"No," the lawyer responded quickly. John tipped his hat and walked away. Jessica opened her door and got in the car. John walked over to his door and paused.

"You two have a nice day," John said, tipping his hat again. John got in and closed the door. They pulled away and headed back to New York. A few minutes later, John's cell phone rang. John pulled it out and looked at it. He smiled at Jessica. She shook her head as he answered the phone.

"How's it going, Trip?" John answered.

"Where are you?" Trip asked.

"I was harassing Archibald," John replied. There was silence for a second.

"I just got a call from Archibald's lawyer. He says that you cut the tires on Archibald's car and threatened him," Trip said, wondering how his agent was going to respond to that.

"They accused me of that," John answered. "I told them I picked the knife up off the ground. Of course I didn't tell them that I had thrown it on the ground after I had slashed Archibald's tires." John thought he heard Trip groan.

"And Jessica?" Trip asked, afraid of the answer.

"She observed me," John answered. "She suggested a different slashing motion on the second tire. That slash was more efficient, and it went much more quickly after that."

"And the threats?" Trip asked. His brain felt like it was pounding in his eye.

"I simply told him I was going to get him, Duck, and Kenneth," John replied. John really thought he heard Trip moan on that one. John shrugged and went on. "He said he was going to kill me in front of Jessica and his lawyer. I told him that better men than him had tried, and he tried to attack me." There was a pause on the line, and then, Trip reluctantly asked the question running through his mind.

"Who besides Bruce has tried to kill you?" Trip asked.

"No one," John replied. "At least Bruce did it face to face. Archibald sends someone else to do his dirty work."

"Do you think you can stay out of trouble the rest of the day?" Trip asked, thinking he knew the answer.

"I can try," John replied. "But, you know I can promise nothing." John heard a click and then a dial tone. John turned to Jessica. "I think he hung up on me."

"I can't understand why," Jessica answered with mock sympathy.

5 Years Ago
The Day After the Nightclub

Chapter 33

Dwayne was sitting alone at a table away from all the other patrons. He was staring at his breakfast and getting nervous. He had just told Liz what had triggered him to do everything he had done, and she had excused herself to the ladies' room. Dwayne felt a weight lift off his shoulders as he saw her return. She gave him a knowing smile.

"Thought I'd gone to turn you in," she said-not asked. Dwayne shrugged, trying to play it off. Liz laughed. "I realized that I would be thinking the same thing while I was in there." She paused for a second. "So, I took my time." Dwayne couldn't help but chuckle.

"Are you going to tell me about yours?" he asked partially from curiosity and partially to make sure that he had something on her.

"I would, but it's very personal and traumatic," she said. Dwayne wasn't sure how to take that. "My father did things to me that he shouldn't have, and that's why I take down guys that look like him." Dwayne thought about that for a second.

"But, I look like him," he said. Liz gave him a "don't be silly" look.

"And, I look like your mom," she replied, grinning.

"Yeah, but she never did anything to me. She just didn't stop others from doing things to me," Dwayne said. Liz got a very dark look on her face.

"So, you're saying I wanted my father to do those things to me," she said softly, but fiercely. Dwayne shook his head no, but Liz was already laughing.

"I know what you mean," Liz said, trying to ease the tension. "There's just something about you. I mean, you understand, I can do things with you and tell you things that I can't tell anyone else about."

"So, what happened?" Dwayne asked. Liz shook her head.

"Another time, not now," she answered. "I can think of many things we can do besides that." Dwayne sat back, not sure if he should have trusted her. "I promise that I'll tell you one day." Dwayne nodded, resigned to the fact that she wasn't going to say anything until she was ready. Little did he know he would spend the rest of his life doing what she wanted.

Now
FBI Building, New York, New York

Chapter 34

"Did those prints come back yet?" John asked Chet as he walked through the door. John had called ahead and told Chet how to access the database he wanted all the evidence collected at Dr. Nichols's murder scene run against. Chet gave John a look.

"Hello to you too, John," Chet responded. "It sure is nice to see you."

"Sorry, Chet," John replied. Chet grinned good-naturedly. "Let me guess. You don't get any direct matches only familial matches." Chet grimaced and shook his head.

"No," he said quietly. John lit up.

"You mean we got him?" Chet made a face and shook his head again.

"No, John," Chet replied. "There are no matches to any of the evidence you had brought in to anyone on that database." John looked perplexed. He turned to Jessica who looked just as confused as he did.

"You mean the former president's father didn't even show up as a familial match? How is it possible that for a person to live somewhere and not leave any DNA?" she asked.

"He did leave DNA," Chet replied.

"And, it's not a familial match to the president?" John asked again just to be sure he didn't miss something. Chet shook his head no again.

"So Dr. Nichols isn't the former president's father?" Jessica asked.

"That's a possibility," John admitted. Jessica thought about that for a second.

"That implies there are other possibilities," Jessica said, looking John straight in the eye.

"I guess it does," John admitted and walked over to his office. Ron watched the whole thing from his desk, still feeling like an outsider. Chet noticed him and waved him over.

"Ron did a lot of the work on this," Chet said as Ron handed the file to Jessica. Jessica nodded.

"No one's forgotten you, Ron," Jessica said. Ron shrugged.

"I kinda like not getting a bunch of grief," Ron said. Jessica smiled, remembering what he had told her about his assignment down in Miami. "So, what now?" Jessica shook her head.

"I don't know," she admitted, leafing through the file. "There's not much to go on right now, and it's not technically our case since it happened in DC. If John pushed for it, we'd get it, but right now, there's not much we can do. He'll probably do paperwork for a while and then start scanning reports to find something." She stopped and looked at him. "Is there something you'd like us to look at?"

"Maybe," Ron said. Jessica raised an eyebrow, intrigued. "Let me make sure I've got everything together." Jessica nodded.

"I mean you've only gone over that file in your desk about a hundred times since you've been here," she said with a grin. Ron looked a little surprised. "I am a FBI agent, so I do notice some things," she added. Chet chuckled and headed back to his desk. Ron headed back to his desk to look at his file for the hundred and first time. Maybe, just maybe, it was time.

Chapter 35

John was shuffling through mounds of paperwork that had been left from his absence. He knew this was the one thing he did not miss during his time off. He looked around the room and saw Ron sitting at his desk, staring at a file. John went back to work and just knew Ron's eyes were focused on him. He glanced over at the office in which Jessica was in working. Jessica winked at him, cut her eyes over to Ron's desk for a second, grinned, and went back to work. In the reflection of his glass office wall, he could see Ron staring at him. John assumed it would just be a matter of time before Ron said something to him.

An hour passed, and John was about to go nuts. Chet had left to go do something, and John couldn't work with eyes boring into his back. He got up from his desk and walked into Jessica's office for a few minutes to talk to her about what he could make for dinner tonight. A couple of times during the conversation, her eyes cut over to where Ron's desk was, but she said nothing about it. As he walked out of her office, he could feel Ron's eyes on him. John had had enough.

John walked over to Ron's desk and stood there for a second. Ron looked up at him.

"Something wrong, John?" Ron asked.

"I was going to ask you the same thing, Ron," John replied. Ron started to say something, but John just shook his head.

"Can you put it up on the screen?" John asked.

"What are you talking about?" Ron asked, trying to appear innocent.

"Whatever it is that is making you stare at me like you want to ask me out, but are afraid since I'm the hot girl, I'll shoot you down," John replied. Jessica had watched John since he left her office and had heard the entire thing. She stifled a laugh, acted like she had just noticed the two talking, and got up from her desk. She leaned against the door frame of her office, watching the two men.

Ron hesitated, mouthing, "Hot girl?" He shook his head and then began typing something on the computer. A picture came up on Ron's monitor. John looked at it and then up at the big screen. He shook his head.

"No, Ron. The big one," he said, pointing to the huge virtual screen that Chet normally used. Ron looked a bit nervous, but hit a button, and a map of the US flew up on the screen. There were dots all over the map. Some were blue, and some were red.

"What am I looking at, Ron? A presidential electoral map?" John asked.

"No," Ron replied quietly. "This is the map of a serial killer I have been tracking that I wanted to see if you would help me catch." John looked at the map and then back down at Ron. John reached out his hand, and Ron handed him the stack of case files. John took them over to the big table and spread them out. Ron looked confused.

"He likes to see it on paper as well," Jessica called out from her office. John looked up, saw her, and motioned her over. She walked over to the table and looked them over.

"There has to be over a dozen," Jessica said.

"Twenty-eight," Ron replied quietly. John looked over at Jessica. She nodded. John looked back at all the files and then at Ron. John straightened and crossed his arms.

"Your case, your lead," John said to Ron. "Tell me all about it."

Chapter 36

Ron looked nervous. He glanced at John, who was starting to get impatient.

"I thought you said he was good?" John asked Jessica, letting Ron hear what he was saying. Jessica tried not to grin but couldn't help herself.

"With your motivation techniques, it's amazing you didn't become a hall of fame basketball coach," she replied sarcastically. John missed the sarcastic part.

"I'm too stubborn to be a head coach," John replied. Jessica nodded along with the statement, fighting to keep from bursting out laughing. John didn't notice and continued. "I refuse to play anything but full court man to man defense, and sometimes, a zone is needed." He paused, thought, and continued. "That and I always believe you should put a man on the out of bounds man." Jessica rolled her eyes.

"Give it up," she said, exasperated. "That was 1992!" John stood up straight and looked shocked like she had slapped him.

"Never," he said quietly but forcefully. Jessica was trying hard to contain her laughter. Ron looked completely confused. Jessica turned and saw him, and that was it. She burst out into laughter. "I don't see what's so funny," John said, never looking at Ron. Jessica was pointing to Ron. John looked over at him, and nodded. John assumed that Ron didn't understand the story. That wasn't quite true; Ron just really didn't care and wondered what he had gotten himself into.

"The Devils stole my Cats' national championship," John said as if that explained everything. Jessica rolled her eyes again. Ron caught that and began to snicker. John looked confused and then glanced over at Jessica and quickly figured out what was going on. "Why won't you just accept the fact that if they had won that game, they would have won the national championship?"

"Because it wasn't the title game, doofus!" Jessica replied. "It was the national quarterfinals. If it had happened in the title game, then I would agree with you." Chet walked in around this time. He took one glance at Jessica and John, realized from past experience that it was, according to John, some deep and philosophical argument, and headed over to Ron.

"'92 basketball game, the words to that rock song, or did Han shoot first?" Chet asked Ron. Ron looked stunned.

"Han shot first!" John said, not even turning toward Chet. Jessica twisted her head to pop her neck.

"Who cares!" she exclaimed. John's eyebrows shot up.

"Do you two care about my murder case?" Ron asked, trying to steer the talk back to the topic at hand.

"Yes!" they both exclaimed at once, never taking their eyes off each other. They both realized how foolish they looked and stopped. They turned toward Ron to listen. John leaned toward Jessica.

"This isn't over," John said. "We'll continue this when we get home."

"Well, thank God for that," she muttered under her breath. John shot her a look. Ron sighed and shook his head. He had done everything in the world to get to New York to work on this case, and now, he wondered if this is what his mother meant by, "Be careful what you ask for. You might just get it."

Chapter 37

"I think we have a serial killer. I have 28 murders starting here," he said as he pointed to a point on the west coast. "And ending here." Ron pointed at a spot in New York State. "Chronologically, these deaths move from west to east over the years before finally settling in New York State." Ron bent down and typed something on the computer, and only the deaths in New York State remained. "About five years ago, the pattern changed." John gave Ron a sharp look. Ron acknowledged it and continued on. "Up until this point, the murders had been committed only on females with a knife piercing the heart. At this point forward, the murders were either male or female, but both have a knife through the heart and a bullet through the brain." Ron paused.

"Same caliber?" John asked. Ron nodded.

"About two years ago, the striations changed on the bullet," Ron said, pointing to a spot on the map. "It appears that a new gun was used because all the striations match up going forward."

"Any ideas?" John asked.

"Right hand groove," Ron said. John nodded.

"That should narrow it down to several hundred thousand. We've all but got him now," John muttered. Ron smiled and shrugged. Ron's eyes went back to the map, and John's went to the table where all the victims' files were laid out. He studied each name quickly. After a second, he found what he was looking for. Jessica was watching him, not sure what was going on. He caught her glance and gave her a sad smile. Ron continued with his presentation.

"We do have one inconsistency," Ron said. John perked up. "The last death was by stabbing only."

"How are you connecting the stabbings?" John asked.

"The knives are all virtually identical," Ron replied. "I've been told by the lab that they were all made around the same time and looked to be handmade." John whistled.

"Any leads there?" John asked, hopefully, but knew there probably weren't any since Ron had pulled him in.

"No," Ron replied. "I'm sure if we had enough manpower, we could comb the entire west coast and eventually find out who made them. One of the weapons experts here is working with some agents out west to try and match them up, but the problem becomes where do we start searching?" Ron punched something on the keyboard, and the entire map pulled back up. "The first death is here in Nevada," he said, using the pointer to indicate a spot on the map. "Obviously, the killer moved east, but is this where the killer live? Or, did the killer just start killing here by happenstance? If so, where did the killer come from? I've had this little town and the surrounding towns gone through with a fine tooth comb, but nothing. I mean nothing."

"What's your gut tell you on this first kill?" John asked, watching Ron. Ron turned to face John.

"You want my gut reaction?" Ron asked. John shrugged.

"You have no leads, and no one knows this case better than you," John replied. "Gut reactions are fine as long as you don't rule evidence out because they didn't go with your gut feeling." Ron took a deep breath.

"I think the scenario that I gave you that this was the first kill, and it was happenstance is correct," Ron replied. "I think something happened that triggered it."

"Why?" John asked.

"Because something else connects all these kills," Ron replied.

Chapter 38

"The killer has a type," John said, not asked. Ron nodded.

"Most of them do," Ron said. John nodded and smiled.

"That and I looked at the files," John added. Ron smiled.

"I see you became an agent for a reason," Ron quipped. Ron typed something on the computer, and pictures pulled up. Jessica made a noise. John turned to look at her.

"You okay?" John asked.

"All the women… they're so similar," Jessica said, a little shaken. "And, the men… they're all similar."

"The women kinda resemble you," John added.

"And Sam," Jessica said, her eyes narrowing. "Do you have a type?" she asked, as if a challenge.

"Yeah," John admitted. "I apparently want women who want to prove me wrong at any given turn." Jessica, as maturely as possible, stuck her tongue out at him. "You done?" She shrugged, and when he turned his back and faced the monitor, she stuck her tongue out again. John ignored her.

"So, you have women who are killed by being stabbed, men who are killed by being stabbed and shot, and women who are killed by being stabbed and shot," Chet said, trying to talk the case through out loud. John and Ron were both nodding in agreement and turned toward Chet. "Something happened to make this killer change everything."

"Different killer?" Jessica asked. John raised his eyebrows and nodded slowly in agreement.

"Killer had a friend or a partner and couldn't continue, and then, the new killer made their own signature?" John asked, expounding on her thoughts. Jessica nodded. John stood their thinking about what was said, slowly playing it through his head. He looked in Ron's direction before he answered. "It works. It's a good theory. I like it." John picked up something strange in Ron. He liked and didn't like what he heard at the same time.

"No, you don't," Jessica said, pulling John away from studying Ron. Ron was genuinely confused.

"He just said he did," Ron said in John's defense. Jessica smiled.

"You misunderstand," Jessica replied. "He likes the train of thought, thinks it's a solid theory, but just doesn't think it fits this case."

"Then, why would he say he liked it?" Ron asked.

"He didn't want me to hurt him," Jessica replied. Ron turned to look at John. John shrugged and gave a quick nod to tell him Jessica was right.

"Then, what do you like?" Ron asked John directly. John tilted his head and looked at the board, then back at the files and then back at Ron.

"I don't know, but I think the same person is responsible for all of these killings," John said. He studied Ron. Ron liked hearing that. Whatever was bothering him before was gone. John continued, "I'm waiting for the things you left out."

"What makes you think I left anything out?" Ron said. John looked Ron straight in the eyes and slowly turned toward the files. He looked back at Ron. Ron dropped his head.

"I'm not criticizing, Ron," John said. "Everyone here knows I'm in no position to say anything." Chet and Jessica were confused.

"What are we missing?" Chet asked.

"One of the victims," Ron said quietly. "She's my mother."

Chapter 39

"That explains a lot," Chet said. John couldn't help but chuckle. Jessica backhanded him on the shoulder.

"What?" John asked. "The guy did whatever he could to get to work with me. He wanted the best to help him try and find out who killed his mother. I can't help it if I'm in high demand."

"You are so modest," Jessica said, exasperated. John smiled, thinking she had complimented him. He straightened his coat.

"When you're good, you're good," John replied, smiling. Jessica rolled her eyes and groaned. John was confused as usual.

"I wouldn't have said it like you did," Ron began, trying to steer this investigation back. "But, yeah, I did want to come to New York to work on the case."

"You think the killer is in New York," Chet said, not asked. "You wanted to try and track the killer down, and you wanted the FBI's resources."

"So getting me was just a bonus?" John asked, surprised that Ron hadn't wanted to come to New York just to work with him. John was having trouble watching Ron because Jessica was behind John trying not to bust into a fit of laughter.

"Yeah," Ron said, trying to act and sound as convincing as he could. Jessica was trying to control herself, but with that answer, she lost it. John tried to ignore her, but it was very hard since she was slapping him on the back as she laughed.

"You know he can tell if you're lying," Chet said, fighting to keep a straight face but losing horribly. Ron didn't say anything. John just stood there as Jessica continued with her laughing fit, and Ron and Chet fought to not laugh in front of John.

"I could use your help, John," Ron said honestly. John nodded, still embarrassed. Jessica was trying to pat him on the back to tell him he could still work on the case and not to be upset, but she couldn't get any air because she was laughing so hard. John straightened his coat and walked to his office without saying anything. Chet and Ron exchanged looks, but neither had a clue what was going on. John picked up the phone and made a call. He spoke softly where no one could hear him.

"Congratulations," Jessica said softly, finally able to control herself. She had walked up beside Ron, while John was making the call. "He's on your side."

"How do you know?" Ron asked.

"He has to prove now that you need him, and you made a mistake by not asking him to start with," Jessica responded with a grin on her face.

"So, that's how you do it," Chet said, mad at himself for never figuring that one out.

"Remember," Jessica added. "Once he gets on a case, he doesn't let up, no matter where it leads." Ron nodded.

"I need answers," Ron said.

"I hope so," Jessica replied. "A lot of people think they do until they get them, and then..." she trailed off and shrugged. Ron nodded.

"I need to know why," Ron said. "Even it was the wrong place at the wrong time, I need to know." Jessica nodded as they watched John hang up the phone and head back into the room.

Small Restaurant Outside of New Jersey

Chapter 40

The mobster referred to lately as Mr. Brown sat at a table, drinking his morning coffee. The restaurant was deserted, the way he liked it. He was a little surprised to hear the bell above the door go off. He was even more surprised to see Robert Mariotti Jr., the boss known as Duck, walk in.

"Well, what a pleasant surprise," Mr. Brown said. "How are you?" Duck shrugged.

"I've been better," Duck replied. "How about you?" Duck paused and then added, "Mr. Brown." Mr. Brown froze with his cup of coffee halfway to his mouth. Mr. Brown had been given the codename by other mobsters. They had wanted to have Duck taken care of and had offered the leadership to Mr. Brown. The name Mr. Brown had only been known to the group, so the fact that Duck had just referred to him by the moniker, Mr. Brown, meant someone had told Duck what was going on.

"Will you join me?" Mr. Brown asked, gesturing toward the empty chair across from him with his coffee cup.

"So, you don't deny it?" Duck asked. Mr. Brown shrugged his shoulders and made an "eh" face.

"What's there to deny? We both know the business we're in," Mr. Brown replied. "I think what you really want to know is what's going to happen." Duck nodded. "You need to leave this mess with the FBI alone."

"I'm the head of the family. I will do what I want," Duck retorted. Mr. Brown made the "eh" face again and shrugged.

"For now," Mr. Brown answered, peering at Duck over his coffee cup as he sipped it. Duck was furious.

"I have made us the most profitable we have ever been!" Duck almost shouted. Mr. Brown nodded.

"I know," Mr. Brown replied. "That's why I'm not planning on having you taken care of." Duck calmed down a little. "Look, what we don't need is the FBI messing with us. You know what happened a few years ago." Mr. Brown stared at Duck for a second. "You know, some think you might have had something to do with all the top bosses being brought down." Duck smiled. Mr. Brown chuckled.

"Sometimes, it pays to be in the right place at the right time," Duck replied.

"Then do us all a favor," Mr. Brown said. "End this thing with your friends, and leave the feds alone." Duck thought on things for a little while.

"And, if I don't?" Duck asked. Mr. Brown shrugged, took a drink of his coffee, and put the cup down in its saucer.

"Then, someone will have you taken care of," he responded. Mr. Brown held his hand up before Duck could start a tirade. "I'm not saying I want to, but if I don't, someone else will. And, you know better than anyone that it's good to be in the right place at the right time." Mr. Brown looked at Duck. Duck started to chuckle.

"Then, why not take me out regardless?" Duck asked.

"The amount of money we're all making," Mr. Brown answered.

"If I end things with my friends, we won't make as much," Duck replied. Mr. Brown shook his head.

"*You*, won't make as much," Mr. Brown retorted. He pointed at Duck as he said "you." Duck nodded, stood, and offered Mr. Brown his hand. Mr. Brown shook his hand.

"I've got some thinking to do," Duck answered and walked out of the restaurant. As he stood on the sidewalk waiting for his driver to open the door to his car, thoughts ran through his mind. He was the boss, and people needed to listen to him. He would talk to his friends but not to end their relationship. No, he wanted them to help him take down those that wanted him gone. Duck smiled. It was good to be king.

Chapter 41

Trip came into the foxhole and glanced around. Something was up, and he wasn't sure what it was. Chet, Ron, and Jessica were over to one side, talking and studying the computer screen. John was over at a table going through numerous files, making notes. John looked a little irritated, and the other three seemed to be amused by something. Trip thought about asking but knew better. Jessica noticed Trip.

"Trip, what can we do for you?" Jessica asked.

"John called and told me he had a case that he wanted to run by me," Trip answered.

"It's Ron's case," John said, never looking up from the photos. He was scribbling something into a small notebook.

"Let's hear it then, Ron," Trip said. Ron nodded and went over the case with Trip. When he was done, Trip looked annoyed.

"Have I done something wrong, sir?" Ron asked.

"No," Trip answered. "It's not you." Trip turned to John. "How did this get missed?"

"There are, what?" John began looking through the files. "Fifteen to twenty states involved. No one was killed in the same city." John pointed toward New York. "The deaths are all around New York City, and only one is inside, so unless someone was looking, they probably never would have seen the connection. Too many overworked investigators with little or no evidence to follow with other bodies pilling up from other cases." John shrugged. "It's easy to see how it's missed." John paused and looked at Trip. "Throw in the change in killing ritual," John added, never taking his eyes off Trip as he spoke. Trip started to say something but thought better of it.

"I'm not sure I follow, sir," Ron said.

"Trip is irritated because no one put this together before, Ron," Jessica said. "He's saying good job, in a very roundabout way, but good job." Trip looked over at the two of them and nodded toward Ron.

"Good work, Agent McGuire," Trip said with a small smile. He looked back over at John. "Ron will be running this?" John nodded. Trip looked back at the map and the circle of kills that circled the city. "You think the killer is somewhere within the city." Ron nodded. "Where do you want to start?" Ron had been working so hard trying to get help on the case that he hadn't thought about it.

"If I may, sir," John said to Ron's relief. Everyone looked at John. John pointed at the one kill inside of New York City. "I think that this kill is significant."

"Why's that?" Jessica asked.

"Deviation from the pattern," John replied. "I wouldn't be shocked to learn that the killer lived within a few blocks of where this body was found."

"Anyone got anything better?" Trip asked. It wasn't that Trip thought John was wrong; it was just the opposite. Trip loved nothing more than John being wrong; it just didn't happen often. Everyone shook their heads. "Then, I guess we know where you're going to start at." Chet, Ron, and Jessica started to leave, but John didn't.

"You guys go ahead," John said. "You three have proven you do fine without me. Besides, I need to talk to Trip about something." Trip gave John a sideways look.

"Okay," Jessica said, a little puzzled. "See you later." The three exited the foxhole. Trip turned toward John, bemused.

"Okay," Trip said. "What is it that we need to talk about?"

"I don't think Ron knows how big this case is," John replied.

Chapter 42

"Any reason you didn't share this with your team?" Trip asked.

"Two," John responded. He dug a file out and tossed it to Trip. Trip leafed through it couldn't figure out the significance until he glanced at the name. He gave John a sharp look.

"Yep," John said to the unasked question. "It's his mother." Trip didn't look happy. "Oh, come on, Trip. It's not like I've never investigated murders I had no business being associated with." Trip gave John a wry smile.

"What is the other reason?" Trip asked and then quickly held up a hand. "Wait, let me guess. You don't like that the killer changed the pattern." John smiled and pointed a finger at him.

"Bingo," John replied. "There's something else. The type of gun changed."

"I don't see the significance of that," Trip said. "There are many reasons to change weapons."

"I agree," John said. "But, look at the big picture." Trip looked up at the board. John went to the computer, typed a few things, and looked surprised when the screen did exactly what he wanted it to.

"I'm telling Chet," Trip said.

"Don't," John replied. "He'll want to throw a party or something." Trip chuckled.

"What are we looking at?" Trip asked.

"The last kill with the old gun," John said, pointing at the circle around the city.

"What about it?" Trip asked.

"Look," John said, pointing at the board. Trip looked and couldn't figure out what John was talking about.

"I don't see it," Trip said.

"Since the killings started in the New York area-" John said, pointing to the half circle, that was pre-gun change.

"They're nearly identical in distance from the city," Trip said, wondering how John saw these things so easily.

"Yep, now look at the last kill with that gun," John said. Trip looked at the board and noticed this kill was closest to the city if you excluded the murder with the knife only.

"Something happened there," Trip said. John nodded. Trip turned to John.

"What did happen there?" Trip asked. John shrugged. "What else am I missing?" John turned to his boss and smiled the knowing smile that irritated everyone.

Chapter 43

"It goes back to the weapon change," John said. He walked over to the files and pulled out his notebook. "The first kill with the knife and the gun was a male. The ME believes he was killed with the gun and then stabbed with the knife postmortem." John watched Trip who was reading the file. Trip nodded to go on.

"The next kill was a female who was killed with a knife, and the ME on this case believes that she was shot postmortem," John said, watching Trip.

"Why go to that trouble?" Trip asked. John shrugged, but the grin on his face told Trip that John had an idea. "Go on."

"It all alternates back and forth until this kill that we talked about earlier," John said, pointing to the one close to, but not in, New York City.

"What happened?" Trip asked.

"The shot didn't kill him," John answered. Trip gave a low whistle.

"Do you think that's why the gun was changed?" Trip asked. John shrugged.

"It could explain everything," John replied, still studying the file.

"What is it?" Trip asked.

"It could be nothing," John said, thinking it was something.

"Go with it," Trip said, a little exasperated.

"Until this victim," John started, gesturing toward the other files, "the victims didn't have what one would call professional jobs. They were waiters, gas attendants, college students, and the like. None of them were nine to five or had completed any professional training." John looked at Trip who nodded. "This one was a marriage counselor." Trip looked at John, wondering what he was about to say. John grinned. "The police got a court order and found the books on the counselor. They got in touch with every couple but one. They left someone to sit on the practice and every couple showed up but one. The Johnsons."

"Fake name?" Trip asked, not believing how quickly John had broken this case. John nodded. "Fake address?" John nodded again. "You aren't suggesting that the killers are married, are you?" John shrugged. Trip looked back at the board and pointed where the first murder with a knifing and gunshot took place. He tapped his finger on his lip as he looked at the map. Something was running through his mind, but it would be preposterous.

"Do you think that these kills," Trip began, pointing at the female kills in which only the knife had been used. "Were done by one suspect?" He looked at John. John was grinning.

"Which means, somewhere there may be a trail of murder victims, probably men, shot in the head," John said. Trip looked at the board.

"You're testing him," Trip said, not asked. John shrugged.

"Right now, Ron is interested in getting justice on the person that killed his mother," John replied. "My guess is only one person is responsible for that murder."

"You're going to let him bring whoever killed his mom to justice, while you concentrate on this second person, if they exist," Trip said, looking at the board. "That way he doesn't get caught in an exhaustive hunt that may or may not exist, but we both suspect does?" Trip looked at John. John nodded.

"John, I don't say this often. You're a good man."

"Aw, shucks, Trip. I'm blushing," John replied. Trip looked back at the map and the murder of the female with only a knife within New York City.

"If you're right, then only one of them was involved with that killing," Trip said, pointing to the spot he had been studying. John nodded. "And, you think that is the killer that killed Ron's mom." John gave a slight shrug, but after a minute, he nodded. Trip continued to study the map, tapping his finger on his lip. Trip stopped, clapped John on the shoulder, and walked out of the foxhole. John got his notebook out and got back to work. He stopped when he realized he was going to have to do a computer search by himself if he didn't want Chet or Ron to know what was going on.

"Nice guys do finish last," he said out loud to himself.

Site of Knife Murder
New York, New York

Chapter 44

Ron, Chet, and Jessica arrived at the spot where the stabbed female victim was found. They looked around the area and decided to put feet to pavement. For the next several hours, they began to show the picture of the young lady to people in the neighborhood, doing an apartment by apartment questioning. It was about four hours in when they questioned Dwayne Sapp about the killing.

"I'm sorry, ma'am, but I've never seen her before," Dwayne lied. There was no trace of the dishonesty on his face or in his body language. Jessica didn't have any internal alarms that Dwayne was a killer. In fact, she found him charming and engaging.

"Have you any idea why someone might leave a body in this neighborhood?" Jessica asked.

"No, not really," Dwayne answered. "I mean, there is that club over there." Dwayne pointed in the general direction.

"Really," Jessica replied. "All I saw were warehouses." Dwayne smiled and shook his head.

"You know how it is," Dwayne replied. "People turn those things into clubs all the time. There's probably ten in a ten block radius in this area." Dwayne smiled. "I won't lie. That's one of the reasons I moved here."

"Oh?" Jessica replied.

"Let's just say I got out of a bad relationship and got tired of not being allowed to have any fun. My marriage counselor recommended I do something for myself now," Dwayne replied with a wry smile on his face.

"So you live here alone?" Jessica asked. Dwayne nodded.

"Just me," he replied.

"Well, I won't bother you," Jessica replied. "Thank you for all your help."

"I helped?" Dwayne asked.

"Yes, you certainly did," Jessica replied. "I've got a lot of research to do to figure out where all of these clubs are located, but I have somewhere to start. If you think of anything, please give me a call."

"Best of luck," Dwayne said, accepting her card. Jessica turned and headed down the hall to the stairs. Dwayne shut the door, feeling a rush he hadn't felt but once since he was married. The FBI had visited and walked away. They had no idea. Liz and her meticulous way of doing things like having a kill room and driving the body to a predetermined location had left him feeling trapped. Didn't she understand that her methods took all the fun out of it? All of the release? All of the pleasure? Dwayne walked into the spare bedroom and looked at the wig, makeup kit, and glasses. The agents could ask around, but they'd never find him. In the years since his first kill, Dwayne had known the importance of disguise. When he went out on kills, he wore shoes with built in lifts. He wore makeup and a wig when he went out to pick up his victim. When he was living his everyday life, he slouched when others were around, giving him the appearance of being even shorter than he actually was. Very few people paid attention to Dwayne. If he talked to someone, he was quite charming, but there was nothing special about him that would make a person remember him. Dwayne had made being disguised in plain sight an art form.

Chapter 45

Dwayne was happy to be by himself. There was no reasoning with Liz, and he had almost learned that the hard way. He had no desire to end up like their marriage counselor or her father. Dwayne scoffed at the thought. For years, Dwayne believed that her father had beaten her, treated her badly, or even, God forbid, molested her. What had Liz's father done that was so horrible? He told her no. When she wanted to do something like camp out all night for tickets for a concert at the age of twelve, he had said no. When she had wanted a brand new sports car when she turned sixteen, he had said no. And for that, she killed him and anyone that had the misfortune of resembling him. She murdered him in a room in the basement with his own handgun. She shot him right in the head, all because he said no.

Dwayne knew deep down something was wrong with himself, but Liz…Liz was stone-cold crazy. Dwayne shook his head when he remembered the one time he had seen Liz lose it. She demanded all their kills be in their own personal, private, sound-proof kill room. The only time she had broken that rule was when she went crazy over their marriage counselor. Dwayne was thankful he had been carrying his knife that day, or there was no telling what might have happened.

In the counselor's private home, Liz had lost it, drew her gun, and fired. It was the first time he ever saw her break her own rule about a spontaneous kill, but it was because the counselor had told Liz that she was too demanding in some things in her marriage. When Liz rebutted that she was the one who kept the marriage together, the counselor had told her, "No." There was probably more coming, but Liz had reached into her purse, drawn out her gun, and shot the counselor. The counselor, not being tied down like all their previous victims, had moved. He had moved much, but it was enough. The shot didn't kill him, and Dwayne had to leap up and stab him to complete the kill. They had managed to keep the bleeding on the rug, and were able to destroy it away from the body. Liz was so enraged that she just dumped the body instead of taking it to the prearranged place Liz had picked out for their next kill.

Dwayne knew that was the beginning of the end. Later that week, Dwayne killed for the first time by himself since he was married. In their world, that was the same as having an affair. Dwayne loved the feeling and knew he had to make a change. It wasn't too long after that he rented the current apartment he was living in. He knew it was close to the previous kill zone, but that was part of its charm. Liz would have hated the idea, which gave it even more appeal. He kept living with Liz and trying to work on their marriage, but he knew in his mind that it was over.

Dwayne glanced at the window and noticed it was getting late outside. He had been so wrapped up with his thoughts that he hadn't realized how much time had passed. He began to prepare for the evening. He was going to kill tonight; he just had to. He knew he was safe from the agents, and frankly, he didn't care. As he began to don the disguise a sense of relief and anticipation that he hadn't felt in a very long time coursed through him.

Chapter 46

Dwayne entered the club shortly after finishing his disguise and found a table that allowed him to look over the patrons. He hadn't eaten. He felt the hunger kept him sharp and on alert. He saw many different women that were all possible candidates, but tonight he was looking for one, a little younger. Not jailbait. No, he wanted one that was college age. He wanted one that was old enough to know what was going to happen to her when it was time. He had found the perfect kill spot a few blocks away. There was a roof top of a parking garage that was deserted this time of night.

Dwayne watched the people come and go. There were so many possibilities, but they just weren't quite right. He watched couples dance together, and he wondered if he was really ever in love. He wondered if he could really feel love, or if he married Liz because he thought she understood him. Did someone like him or Liz deserve happiness? Dwayne chuckled to himself. Who cared? Who cared what he was allowed to deserve, or if he could feel love. There was one thing he could feel, the rage. He felt it burrowing it through him. He felt the taste in his mouth he always got before he killed. It was a high for him. His breathing increased, he felt euphoric, and then, he froze. He froze for just a second. Something wasn't right. He just knew it. He carefully checked his surroundings, but there was no one watching him. Maybe the visit by the FBI had spooked him more than he thought.

Dwayne thought about calling the whole thing off. It was better to be cautious than get caught. That was what Liz had told him countless times. Just thinking about Liz made him angry and determined. That's when he saw her. She was perfect: right age, right height, right color hair, just absolutely perfect. Dwayne watched as she had to run guys off one after another. Dwayne smiled and moved in for the kill. He walked up to her table, and put out his hand.

"Hi," Dwayne began. "I'm Bill." The woman shook his hand, hesitantly. "Look, I'll be brief. I came in here tonight just to get out of the house. I've seen at least five guys hit on you, and it's obvious that you have no want to have one of those type of nights." The lady looked at him, intrigued as to where he was going. "I'm not looking for a hook up or a date. I'm simply offering to sit here and help you ward off those wanting to court you." The lady smiled.

"That's a heck of a pick-up line," she responded. Dwayne shook his head.

"No line," he responded. "I'll go if you want me to." She shook her head.

"No, feel free to stay," she responded. "All I wanted to do was get out of the house without being chased by every available person here." She paused, held out her hand, and continued. "Hi, my name is Amanda."

John's and Jessica's Apartment
New York, New York

Chapter 47

"How was your day, honey?" John asked as Jessica dragged her way through the apartment door.

"Exhausting," Jessica said. John raised an eyebrow; she had spoken in more of a whine.

"That's so unbecoming of you," John replied. Jessica fell on the couch. John walked over to the couch, picked up her legs, sat under them, took her shoes off, and began to rub her feet. Jessica closed her eyes and made a guttural moan.

"I knew I married you for some reason," Jessica mumbled.

"That's why you're a master detective," John responded. "You stayed on the case until you figured out what I was good for."

"Shut up and keep rubbing, detective boy," Jessica retorted. John did as he was told.

"So, did you find out anything?" John asked after a few minutes of silence. Jessica groaned.

"Why must we talk about this?" Jessica asked. John shrugged, took his hands off her feet, and sat back. Jessica opened her eyes and sat up. "You wouldn't!" John looked at her with feigned innocence and shrugged.

"My hands hurt," he said, trying not to grin. She feel back, and shut her eyes. John's hands carefully enclosed one of her feet, rubbed for a few seconds, and stopped.

"Okay! Okay!" she yelled. "I'll tell you anything! Just keep rubbing!" John began to rub again. "I found out that there are many clubs in the area where the body was dumped."

"Chet's the best," John said.

"Wasn't Chet," Jessica responded, sighing deeply.

John slowed down the rubbing. "I mean, he did find out where they are all located at in the area. It's late, and we decided to hit them tomorrow. No, the tip was given by some guy that lived in the area!" she added quickly. John resumed.

"Young party boy?" John asked. Jessica chuckled.

"Nope," she replied. "He's actually closer to your age. He moved in the area after he and his wife split. His marriage counselor recommended he do something for himself, so he moved into the area." John stopped rubbing. "I told you everything, I swear!" John put her feet down, got up, went to the closet, and pulled out her running shoes. "Whatever I did, I'm sorry!" John brought the shoes over to her.

"Put these on," he said, an urgency in his voice. Jessica recognized the tone and popped up off the couch.

"I need socks with those. I can just put the ones I was wearing," she replied.

"No good," John said. "We're going clubbing, and I don't want you whining all night that your feet hurt."

"I can't go out dancing in these clothes with those shoes!" Jessica exclaimed.

"We're not going dancing," John replied. "There was a kill that was off the pattern that had been established, and it was a marriage counselor." Jessica stared at John thinking. "How many guys do you know that are my age that want to move into an area where the clubs run all hours of the night?"

"Not everyone is as old and as much of a fuddy duddy as you are," Jessica replied, still irritated about her foot rub ending. John looked at his hands and then at her feet. "Don't make me lie to you because I will if that's the only way I can get a foot rub."

"At least you're honest," John replied, shaking his head. "Look, if I'm wrong, I'm sorry, but do you want to chance it?" Jessica went and got socks. She came back with the socks on. Defeated, she grabbed the shoes, put them on, and glanced in the full length mirror at her outfit. She turned toward John with a look of disgust on her face.

"You look beautiful," John said.

"Two things," Jessica began. "You think I'm hot in sweats." John nodded in agreement. "Two, we're married. You're kinda obligated to tell me I look beautiful, no matter what."

"I can't lie without breaking into hives," John replied. Jessica thought for a second and beamed at him.

"Let's go catch a killer," she said. "We've got things to do tonight."

"You mean I have to rub your feet some more," John said, not asked.

"Yeah," she said like he was an idiot, disappearing out the door.

Amanda
Night Club

Chapter 48

"I've lived a life of lies," Amanda said to the man she thought was Bill. Well, shouted was the better word. The music was blaring, and Amanda could hardly hear herself think. "My father isn't who I thought he was. He may have even killed my grandfather!"

"I'm sorry," Dwayne said, trying to appear to be intently listening. Amanda shrugged.

"I barely knew him," Amanda admitted. "What I thought about my family wasn't true, and the only person that seems to care about me isn't even blood related."

"That's rough," Dwayne said, feeling something right between his shoulder blades. It was like someone was boring a hole through them. He moved his shoulders, uncomfortable, and glanced around to see if anyone was watching him. He didn't see anyone. When he turned back to Amanda she looked concerned.

"Are you okay?" she asked.

"I'm fine," Dwayne responded. "I just feel like someone is staring at me." Amanda glanced around.

"I don't see anyone," she said. "Do you want to get out of here?"

"Sure," Dwayne said.

"I know a great place we can go have coffee," she said.

"That's fine," Dwayne responded. "You in a coffee mood?"

"Not really," Amanda responded.

"If you want to talk, I know a great place that overlooks the city and is in public so you don't have to worry about me being a creep," Dwayne said with a smile on his face.

"I don't think you're a creep," Amanda replied with her own smile. "I just am not looking for anyone right now. I've got too many father issues."

"Well, and let's not forget the other thing," Dwayne began. Amanda looked slightly confused. "I'm probably old enough to be your father." Amanda laughed. They got up and left. Dwayne could feel the excitement building through him. It wasn't going to be long now. Soon, he would get his release.

They headed out of the club and started walking down the street. In a few minutes, they were at the place Dwayne had told her about.

"I don't know," Amanda said, giving the place a once over.

"Come on," Dwayne urged. "Let's go to the top, and if you don't like it, then we'll go find someplace to get coffee." Amanda nodded, and they headed up to the top floor. Amanda looked over the view of the city. She glanced over at Dwayne who seemed at peace. They talked for an hour about her father in vague terms. Actually, Amanda talked, and Dwayne just listened. He knew it wouldn't be long.

"It's getting a little cold out," Amanda said. "Do you think we might go get that cup of coffee?" Dwayne smiled. Finally, it was time.

"Sure," he replied. "Come on, let's take the stairs." They headed to the stairwell and entered. As they started down the stairwell, Dwayne knew exactly what he was going to do. The next floor down was enclosed, and the chance of anyone being around was next to zero.
"Amanda," he said with fake panic in his voice. "Let's go in this door," he said, pointing at the stairwell door. "I can't shake the feeling that someone is following me." Amanda nodded and headed through the door. Dwayne followed close behind, drawing out the knife he was going to use to finish off her life. Amanda had stopped in front of

him and was looking around, trying to figure out where the best place was to hide so they could confront the person they thought was following them. She was surprised as an arm wrapped around her throat from behind. As Dwayne pulled back the knife, he felt the rage pour though his body. The feeling was absolute ecstasy. He knew the only way to complete it was to kill the young girl in front of him, and that was exactly what he planned on doing.

John and Jessica
Night Club

Chapter 49

"Whose brilliant idea was this again?" John asked, watching the sea of humanity dancing, jumping, and doing things that he would have called having a fit. John and Jessica had already visited the apartment of their witness and couldn't locate him. This was the fifth nightclub they had visited. They had gotten a copy of the tenant's picture and were now showing it, along with the murder victim's picture, at each club.

"Yours, master detective," Jessica responded.

"What are they doing, and is it legal?" John asked.

"I believe it's called twerking," Jessica replied.

"Why would anyone do that?" John asked. Jessica looked at him with a smile and shook her head. "Dare I ask?"

"Nope," Jessica said, heading toward the bartender. She flashed her badge at him. John saw him immediately change his demeanor.

"Look," John said. "I don't care what's going on here. I just want to catch a killer. Do you know this man?" he asked, drawing a photo out of his jacket pocket. The bartender looked at the photo and then back at John.

"Sir, no disrespect, but I don't think that's a man," the bartender said. "I have seen her though." Jessica grabbed the photo.

"You showed him the picture of the victim, didn't you?" she asked as she glanced at the photo. She did a double take and was surprised on two fronts. John watched her.

"What?" John asked.

"Are you absolutely sure you saw her?" Jessica asked, praying he was wrong.

"Yeah, she left here not half an hour ago," the bartender said. John got the picture from Jessica and saw it was Amanda. John swallowed.

"Was she tweaking?" John asked through gritted teeth. The bartender looked confused. Jessica closed her eyes, trying not to laugh.

"Twipping, torqueing, twapping? Whatever it's called!" John yelled. The bartender backed up a step.

"Was she twerking?" Jessica asked as calmly as possible. John nodded and pointed at Jessica as if to say, "What she said." He was visibly upset.

"No," the bartender answered. "She came in and got a soda. I don't remember what kind. She was hit on by about five guys until someone she must have been waiting for showed up. They talked for a while and then left."

"Was it the former President of the United States?" John asked seriously. The bartender looked at John like he was the village idiot. Jessica shook her head.

"What? No." the bartender answered. Jessica reached over to John's coat and pulled out the other two pictures. John tried to protest but was still too upset about the potential twerking episode to say anything that made sense.

"Do you recognize either of these two people? One of them may have been from a long time ago," Jessica asked, showing him the photo of Dwayne and of the murder victim. The bartender looked at Dwayne and shook his head. He then looked at the murder victim.

"I don't know this guy," the bartender answered. "But, this lady, yeah. I remember her because she was killed, wasn't she?" Jessica nodded. The bartender looked back at the photo, made a face. "In fact, she was talking to the same guy that the girl in the earlier photo was." John snapped his head up and studied the bartender. He was telling the truth.

"Are you sure?" Jessica asked, concerned. "That was a long time ago."

"I'm sure," the bartender answered, nodding. Jessica gave him her card.

"Call me if you think of anything else" she said. The bartender nodded and went back to work. "Now what?" she asked John. A dancing club patron bumped into John.

"Seriously," John said. "Why?" Jessica grabbed John and dragged him out of the club.

"Come on, fuddy duddy," she said. "Let's go find Amanda, and then, if you give me a really good foot rub, I can teach it to you."

"Why?" John asked.

"So I can have a good laugh," she replied.

Chapter 50

John and Jessica continued to look around the neighborhood, trying to find where Amanda might have gone. They showed her picture around, and someone said she had headed down the street with some man. John and Jessica headed down the street, trying to find anyone who might have seen her. John and Jessica passed what appeared to be a drunk homeless man in an alley. They were across from a parking garage.

"Hold up," John said. "He might have seen something."

"He definitely might have," Jessica replied. "It smells like a distillery. There's no telling what he saw."

"Trust me," John said. John walked over to the man slumped in the alley. He showed the man his badge. "Have you ever seen this girl?" he said, showing him the picture.

"Nopppee," the man slurred. John got down close to him. Jessica made a face, imagining the smell from that close.

"I don't want to break your surveillance," John whispered. "But, this is important." The man looked at Jessica and gave her a nod with his head to the left. Jessica, confused took a step to the left, shielding the drunk in case anyone looked into the alley.

"I've been watching that building over there for drug deals for over a month," the man whispered, all traces of a slur gone. "I saw her and some man go in about an hour ago. Someone followed them in there; I couldn't tell if it was a man or a woman."

"I'll give you fifty dollars if you can just tell me if you saw her," John said loudly, so if anyone were around they would think the man was a bum.

"Thanks," the man whispered. "How'd you make me?"

"I've been undercover myself," John replied. "The

smell is a little too strong for you not to be passed out."
Jessica was amazed. "Also, I notice things. Trust me. No
one else would have picked up what I did." The man
started to say something when a scream pierced the night.
John jumped up and ran toward the parking garage.

"Do you need me?" the man asked Jessica fiercely
but quietly. She shook her head, beginning to start after
John.

John ran up each level, checking them as he went.
When he got to the third floor and opened the door, his
heart leapt into his throat. He had his gun out, pointing
toward the bodies he saw lying there. A man lay on the
ground, with Amanda on top of him. Off to the side sat
another lady on her heels. She was sobbing uncontrollably.

"She killed him," the woman kept saying over and
over. John looked at the bodies. The man laid there; blood
had obviously poured out of his chest. John saw the knife
that had been sticking out of his chest. John didn't know
for sure, but he was pretty sure it was the exact match for
all of the knives in those cases that Ron had shown him.
What troubled John the most was the knife was in
Amanda's hand. As Jessica burst into the room, John
turned to her. A lost look covered his face. Jessica nodded
and took over the scene, knowing her husband's heart had
metaphorically been stabbed just like man that lay on the
ground.

Chapter 51

Jessica stepped to the body and checked the pulse of the man on the floor. She shook her head. John closed his eyes. She moved to check Amanda's pulse. She looked up at John and nodded.

"She's alive," Jessica said. John nodded and quickly bent over, feeling nauseous. Jessica started to check on him when she noticed movement in the corner of her eyes. The woman on the ground had her hands folded in a way that it was impossible to tell if anything was in them. She had stood suddenly, and it was obvious that she had a small gun in her hands. With one quick look, Jessica was sure the gun was similar to the one that had fired the bullets in the murder cases they had been investigating.

"She killed him!" the woman screamed. "I was going to kill him! I was going to kill him for everything he made me do! He used me! He used me!" The woman had her gun pointed at Amanda. Jessica stepped into the line of fire, her own gun up and pointed at the armed woman. She started to speak when she was interrupted.

"Put! The gun! Down!" John yelled, his gun aimed at the woman with the gun. Jessica glanced at John, and she didn't know if she had ever seen that level of intense rage on his face except when he had fought Bruce. "Lady, this isn't the time or place!" John yelled. "Drop it, or I drop you!"

"John!" Jessica shouted. "Stand down!" John blinked in confusion and started to lower his weapon. The lady with the gun had already put her arms down to her side and had sunk to her knees, crying. Jessica kept her gun trained on the lady and had one hand pointed toward John in a stop gesture. John didn't know what to do. Jessica felt for him, but right now, the only important thing was securing the weapons and the crime scene. The door to the stairwell flew open, and the man that had been disguised as a bum came in, weapon drawn. He stepped forward and saw the scene.

"Holy," he began, but trailed off. "It looks like this place is going to be shut down for a while." He pulled out a phone and started to call in an ambulance. John shook his head. The man nodded and called in a coroner. Jessica had taken the weapon away from the sobbing lady.

"What's your name?" Jessica asked, trying to get control of the scene.

"Elizabeth Sapp," she replied through the sobs. "The dead man is my husband, Dwayne." She paused. "He's murdered dozens of people over the years. He's a very bad man. For a while, he made me help him, but then all of a sudden, he didn't want me with him anymore." She began to cry again, and Jessica looked at John. John was staring at Elizabeth. He looked at Jessica and nodded. She was telling the truth, at least what she considered the truth to be. Elizabeth took a deep breath. "I think he's been killing again without me, and this girl could be helping him." John quickly looked over at Elizabeth, but he couldn't tell anything. He had missed his chance. He looked at Amanda lying there and couldn't help but wonder. If her father was as evil as John thought he was, then was it possible that Sam's daughter was more like Kenneth than John thought. Was she truly like father, like daughter?

Chapter 52

Jessica put on gloves and carefully took the knife out of Amanda's hands. John was kneeling near Amanda, conscious of the blood. John didn't want to contaminate the crime scene. Amanda was starting to stir.

"Ohhh," she moaned.

"Careful," John said quietly. Amanda opened her eyes and looked at John. She then looked at Dwayne and jumped backwards. "You need to be still. This is a crime scene now, and you can't mess it up. Do you understand?" Amanda nodded and looked at Dwayne's body.

"He tried to kill me," she said softly, almost in shock.

"That's a lie!" Elizabeth spat and came to her feet. She had a wild look in her eyes and looked ready to attack Amanda. The man dressed as a bum began to move toward Elizabeth, but Jessica got there first. She gently, but firmly grabbed her by both arms. Elizabeth looked Jessica in her eyes for a second and then dropped her head.

"I know you are hurt and angry," Jessica said softly. "But, you have to calm down before you make this worse, Elizabeth."

"Liz," she responded softly. Liz looked at Jessica. Jessica gave her a small smile and nodded. Jessica let Liz go, and Liz sat back down on the ground, the fight apparently gone out of her. Jessica wasn't sure how long that was going to last, but she would take it.

"I'm Hank, by the way," the man dressed as a bum said. "I was undercover, NYPD." Jessica walked over and shook his hand. "Is he okay?" he said, nodding toward John.

"No," Jessica responded. "It's long and complicated. The short version is that lady who has apparently stabbed the victim is his wife's daughter." The undercover cop gave her a sharp look. "I'm going to need your help securing this scene." Hank nodded. Jessica walked over to John. "You need to leave everything alone."

"I told her that," John answered. Jessica placed a hand on his arm.

"Sweetie, I was talking to you," Jessica responded gently. John looked at her, the hurt washing over his face. He looked off into space, gave a slight nod, and stood up.

"I can't work this crime scene," John said to Amanda. "It could get all of us into a lot of trouble. Do you understand?" Amanda nodded and turned toward Jessica. Jessica smiled at Amanda and shook her head slightly.

"I am not going to either," Jessica said. "Personal conflict." Amanda looked confused. "Like it or not, you're my best friend's daughter, and the fact I'm John's wife doesn't help things. We're leaving the crime scene alone, but that doesn't mean we can't help you. We will." Amanda nodded, and Jessica felt Hank hovering behind her. She sighed, grabbed John's arm, and led him away from the scene.

"This is a mess," John said quietly.

"It's a good thing she has the world's best detective on it," Jessica said softly. John turned toward her.

"I don't know -" John began.

"You had best not be about to say you don't know if you can do this," Jessica said with a determined look on her face. "We're going to do exactly what Sam would expect us to do."

"She would want me to do everything I could," John said softly. Jessica nodded. "You know what that means?" John asked. Jessica grinned. John was really beginning to understand why everyone hated his grin.

"You mean unleash everything that is John Fowler?" Jessica asked, the grin growing. "You mean unleash every crazy idea in your mind until you blow this case wide open and prove she didn't do it, although every

indication here is that she did?" John nodded. "Boy, do I."
John grinned. Jessica kissed him. She pulled back and
looked him directly in the eyes. "Go get 'em, Tiger."

Chapter 53

Trip, Ron, and Chet showed up at the scene a few minutes later. Jessica left John and went over to talk to them. John watched Hank talk with Amanda. Hank was treating her well, but John still wished he was able to comfort her. He glanced over at the four talking and noticed them glancing at him. John looked away and gathered himself. It was time. He buttoned his coat, closed his eyes, focused, and thought about Sam.

"This is for you," John said softly. He walked toward the four of his friends. Jessica started toward him, but he barely slowed. "Call the Moores," he whispered to her. She saw the look on his face, and a grin grew. John was really starting to hate that look on other people. Trip started to speak as he approached them. John started before he could.

"Good news, Ron," John began, noticing the look of surprise Trip was giving him. "I think we found your serial killer." Ron looked at John with surprise. John glanced at Trip, who gave the slightest nod of approval. John grinned. He just couldn't help himself. "It looks like the weapon his widow has will match the newer killings since the gun change. I haven't interviewed her yet, but from what she screamed at me, I believe she was part of the killings. She is implying that Dwayne forced her to join in on the killings. Good work, Ron. You just closed almost thirty cases." Ron looked at him. John could tell he was glad it was over, but something was missing. "Trust me when I say shooting the person who took someone from you isn't nearly as satisfying as you dream it would be." Ron studied John for a second and nodded.

"I hate to ask," Ron began and paused.

"You investigate it like you would any murder," John answered. "I will tell you the widow did imply that Amanda may have joined Dwayne on some killings since they split. You'll also find a bartender at a local club that will tell you that Dwayne seemed to meet with Amanda, and she left with him of her own free will." Ron stared at John.

"I'll never understand you," Ron said softly and then looked around uncomfortably, realizing he had said it out loud. John chuckled.

"At least you're honest about it," John said. "Go compare notes with my wife. I guarantee she doesn't understand me either." Ron nodded and started toward Jessica. John gave him a pat on the back to tell him they were fine, and Ron nodded. Chet chuckled at the whole thing and went with Ron. Trip stood there, staring at John.

"I know you," Trip said. John nodded. "What are you up to?"

"As a FBI agent, I go where the evidence leads me," John answered, sticking his hands in his pockets and rocking back on his heels. Trip eyed him.

"And as John Fowler?" he asked. John grinned.

"I do what I do," John answered. Trip smiled.

"And, God help those that get in your way," Trip said, not asked. John grinned and nodded. He looked over at Hank who had finished questioning Liz and Amanda.

"Excuse me a second," John said and headed over toward Hank. Trip went over to where Ron and Chet were talking with Jessica. Hank nodded toward John as he approached. "Learn anything?"

"Maybe," Hank said, guarded.

"I'm going to tell you something you've never heard an FBI agent say to a NYPD officer," John began. Hank looked interested. "I need your help."

Chapter 54

The next morning, John walked into his office. He felt horrible. He had little to no sleep, and he was more than a little upset that Amanda had to spend the night in custody. He did manage to get her into FBI custody after he told Hank what he needed. John made an offer Hank couldn't refuse, and perhaps the first ever deal between local law enforcement and a federal agency was made that both sides were happy with. Hank had loved the idea so much he had worked through the night and had already called John that morning. Hank had already contacted some other people for John to talk to, and John was waiting on their phone calls.

Liz had also been kept overnight. No one was sure if she was a suspect or a witness. John had grabbed the lab reports that lay on Ron's desk, and he was sure she was heading toward being a witness. John's cell phone rang, and he went to his office and did something he never did. He shut the door and continued the conversation in private. As he was finishing up, he saw his friends coming in, and by the look on their faces, he knew that they were worried. John turned his back to them, so they couldn't see him smile. He knew a lot more than they did right now. For one thing, he was investigating a case that was different than theirs.

He finished the call, opened the door to his office, and walked out.

"The Moores know," Jessica said. John nodded. "They want to know if she needs a lawyer?"

"Am I questioning her today?" John asked, looking at the uncomfortable faces on Ron and Chet. John held the grin off that fought to cover his face. He didn't need his ability to be able to read them.

"I don't see why not," Trip said from the doorway. No one had heard him come in.

"At this point, she's still a person of interest?" John asked. Trip nodded. "Then, no lawyer for now." Jessica gave him a hard look. John shook his head slightly and let the grin show on the corner of his mouth.

"You play a dangerous game, John," Jessica said softly.

"I practice every night with my wife," he responded as he walked over to Trip to see the folder he was holding. A touch of color hit Jessica's cheeks, and she lost to the embarrassed smile that made its way on her face.

"I got ten on Jessica," Ron deadpanned to Chet.

"I got a hundred on her," Chet replied.

"You shouldn't be gambling, Chet," John said from the other side of the room. Trip closed his eyes and winced. Jessica made a low whistle. "Are you all through playing so that we go find out what happened?"

"Mrs. Sapp claims that Amanda stabbed the victim," Ron said. John closed the folder, looked at Ron, and nodded.

"Bullets in her gun match the other victims?" John asked. Ron nodded.

"She wants to talk to a lawyer before telling us about her part in the other murders," Ron said. John nodded.

"Lawyer here?" John asked.

"Yep," Ron replied.

"You take another run at her once she talks to the lawyer, but I'm assuming you don't want to charge her on these murders?"

"From the evidence we have so far, no," Ron replied. John nodded.

"I'm going to go question Amanda," John said. Ron and Chet slipped out of the room. John smiled, and turned toward Trip.

"Do you want me there?" Jessica asked. John turned toward her, and shook his head. "Okay," she replied, smiled, and left the room. John turned back to Trip.

"Still testing them?" Trip asked. John shrugged. "They'll eventually put it together." John nodded. "But here's my question. Why are you questioning Amanda if you aren't on this case? The one that you broke last night, if I may add."

"I was simply looking for a clue on another case I was working, and I happened to stumble across their case," John replied.

"And now, you're questioning her about your case," Trip said, not asked. John grinned and nodded. "And, they still have no idea." John shrugged. "What do you think you're going to find?"

"The same thing I am always after, Trip - the truth," John replied as he rocked back on his heels. Trip shook his head.

"You're eliminating her as a suspect," Trip said. "What if you don't?"

"I'll go where the truth leads me," John replied.

"What if the truth is something you can't handle?" Trip asked. John grinned.

"Haven't I proved by now there's nothing I can't handle?" Trip groaned, shook his head, and left. John went and got his notes and headed upstairs to the interrogation room. He stood outside and looked at the door.

"This is for you, Sam," he said quietly.

Chapter 55

John opened the door and walked inside the interrogation room. He knew Chet, Ron, Jessica, and Trip were all on the other side of the glass, watching. Amanda glanced at John. In the brief second he held her eyes and could study her face, he read conflicting emotions: contempt and hope. Amanda still didn't trust John, and given her circumstance, John didn't blame her. But, what surprised John was the hope. Why would seeing him inspire hope inside of her? Could it be he was finally getting through to her?

"I didn't do it," she said simply. John studied her and slowly nodded. She didn't. He could read it on her. She didn't do this. Now, how did he convince the others?

"I believe you," John said. Amanda just stared at John. It was a mixture of disbelief and the thought that John was lying. "I'm serious, but I need your help getting you out of this mess."

"You could get me out of this," she said softly. "My father would get me out of this."

"Do you really want to discuss your father right now?" John asked. When John received no answer, he continued. "I can't find that you're even related to the man you say you are." Amanda smiled and leaned forward.

"He's not going to have his DNA where just anyone can get to it," she responded.

"It's not where you're implying it's at either," John countered. Amanda sat back. John expected to see surprise, but what he saw was disappointment. "Why not?" Amanda just looked at John for a second.

"Are you trying to flip me, or whatever it is you call it?" she asked.

"No," John answered, shaking his head quickly. "I just need to establish some stuff. If everything can't be proven, how am I supposed to get anyone to trust you?" Amanda sat there, studying John. John couldn't help himself; he began to grin, which only seemed to irritated Amanda.

"What?" she asked. John tried to quit, but the grin only grew.

"Your mother," he answered softly. "When she was trying to figure out if there was some hidden meaning in my statements, she would give me the same look and play stuff back in her mind."

"So, my mother didn't trust you?" Amanda asked. The grin fell from John's face immediately. He became flustered and wasn't quite sure how to answer when he noticed she had a grin of her own. The same self-satisfied grin Sam used to get when she would one up him. John started to laugh until tears appeared in his eyes. What Amanda didn't know was the tears were a mixture of the laughter and the worry of how disappointed Sam was going to be if John didn't get her daughter out of this mess.

Chapter 56

John was trying to figure out how to gain Amanda's trust when Amanda leaned in. John leaned in as well. Amanda talked very softly so as not to be overheard by those in the other room.

"My father's DNA is probably not on file anywhere for national security reasons," she said, looking John directly in the eye.

"President Nichols's DNA is on file. It just doesn't match yours as a familial match," John answered just as softly.

"I know," Amanda said, not happy with that fact.

"Is it Rich's?" John asked. Amanda's head snapped back, shocked. Her mouth slightly dropped open from the surprise. It wasn't necessary for Amanda to answer now. John knew the truth, and the final piece to that puzzle slid into place in his head. It all made sense to him now. If it ever came out about Amanda and how she was conceived, Kenneth could have his DNA submitted and found innocent. That was probably an added bonus to go along with the fact that no one could ever pin any crime anywhere on Kenneth where DNA evidence was involved. Something hit John suddenly, and he made a slight note on his paper, not that he could forget what he was thinking.

"How do you know about him?" Amanda asked, a cross between fury and admiration running across her face.

"Because I'm the best," John said. "As that guy says on the song, it's not bragging if you can back it up." Inside the observation room, Chet groaned, Jessica smacked her head with her palm, and Trip just chuckled.

"He's all yours, Jessica," Trip said, still chuckling. Jessica shot Trip a look, which did nothing but encourage him.

"Seriously, how did you find out?" Amanda asked John back in the interrogation room.

"I've got some friends in high places," John answered. "How do you propose we get you out of this mess?" he asked, trying to change the subject.

"Well, you have no witnesses," Amanda began.

"We have Liz Sapp," John countered.

"The victim's wife who has said she helped him in the murders," Amanda replied.

"She said she was forced," John responded.

"She said she thought she had to help, or he might kill her," Amanda countered. John had to give her that point.

"I saw you holding the knife," John said.

"I was trying to save his life, even after he tried to kill me," Amanda said.

"So, you pulled it out?" John asked.

"I don't know," Amanda answered. "She had a gun. She yelled at him as he was about to slit my throat, and he turned. That's when I grabbed the knife. He hit me in the head with the knife. The whole world started spinning, and I did the only thing I knew to do. I kicked him in the groin."

"That can cause someone to pause in their tracks, but that doesn't tell me how he got stabbed," John replied. Amanda shrugged.

"I know I managed to grab it, but what happened next, I have no idea. I'm pretty sure I passed out. When I woke up, she was sitting in the floor sobbing, and I was covered with blood. The knife was in my hand."

"Your prints are over his on the handle," John said softly. Amanda nodded. "That shows you were the last person to hold the knife."

"I've already told you that," Amanda replied, frustrated. "He's a serial killer, and he's dead."

"Stabbed exactly where numerous other victims have been stabbed," John said. "I'm not saying this is what happened, but it could be argued that you helped him or even murdered some of those men yourself."

"Or, Liz could have," Amanda replied, get angrier by the minute.

"There's no evidence to support that," John said. Amanda shook her head.

"There's my word," Amanda said. John nodded and started to reach across the table to take her hand. Amanda jerked her hand back as John stopped himself. There was an uncomfortable silence in the room for a few seconds. The four in the interrogation room all looked at each other and had their own uncomfortable silence. John cleared his throat.

"Do you have any ideas that could help me?" John asked.

"Yes," Amanda answered, sitting upright and looking John right in the eye. "Go and make any evidence they have against me disappear."

Chapter 57

Two hours later Trip, Ron, Jessica, Chet, and John met in Trip's office. It would have been sooner, but John said he had something to take care of. Jessica followed John from a safe distance and got a little worried when he went to the DNA lab, but John never came close to the evidence in Amanda's case. He did manage to lose her for a few minutes. Actually, she never would have found him if he hadn't tapped on her shoulder from behind.

"Satisfied I didn't mess with the evidence?" John asked after Jessica calmed down from being startled.

"John, I, I mean," Jessica sputtered.

"It's fine, Jess," John replied. "I would have had me followed too."

"Where were you?" she asked.

"I had a phone call to take," John answered. Jessica gave him a strange look but let it go.

When they met in Trip's office, John was sure it was going to be four against one about what to do, but he really didn't care. He knew Amanda was innocent, and he knew what he owed Sam. John decided, as usual, to just jump right in.

"She's innocent, Trip," John said, knowing he had just cranked the uncomfortableness in the room up about 4 notches. "I saw it on her face. She didn't kill him."

"John, if this was any other person would you feel this way about letting her go?" Trip asked.

"If it was anyone else in lock up, would you doubt that I was right?" John countered. Trip thought for a second. He looked to Chet. Chet nodded. Trip glanced to Jessica who nodded as well. When Trip looked to Ron, Ron just shrugged. John laughed. "What about you, Trip?"

"You're right," Trip admitted. "But, they'll eat us alive if we let her go."

"I know," John said. Jessica sank into a chair, shocked. Chet shook his head like he had misheard. Trip looked like an aneurysm had begun. Only Ron vocalized what everyone else was thinking.

"Wait, you know Trip's right and are agreeing she needs to be locked up?" Ron asked, flabbergasted. "Then, why are you in here?"

"To make sure this investigation proceeds," John replied.

"You think Trip wouldn't let us keep looking into it?" Ron asked, still confused.

"No," John answered. Jessica was mumbling something about having married an idiot. "You have," John said, shooting Jessica a smile. John turned back to everyone else. "I just want to make sure I wasn't seeing something I wanted to see."

"What do you want to do?" Trip asked, head still hurting.

"I have no idea," John answered. He looked down at the floor for a second and then back up. "All I know is I can't let Sam's kid go to jail for something she didn't do."

"That's what this is all about," Jessica said. Trip looked over at her. "You think this is your chance to make up for her dying?" John looked away, not trusting himself to answer.

"Close the door, Ron," Trip said. "We've got to figure something out to help this girl and do it in a manner we can all sleep at night." John looked back at Trip and nodded his thanks.

Chapter 58

As Ron went to close the door, the tech that John had talked to earlier appeared in the doorway.

"Yes?" Trip asked.

"I'm sorry, sir," the tech began. "I was looking for Agent Fowler." John turned around and saw the tech.

"Is it done already?" John asked, surprised.

"No, not yet, sir," the tech replied. "Is it okay to use the new machine? It's much faster to make the comparisons in it."

"Will it hold up in court?" John asked. Jessica gave John a look. What was he up to?

"It can tell you that there is a one in a one quadrillion chance that someone else might have the same DNA. We've never had a judge disallow it. Plus, with you moving up to the front of the line with your special task force request, it shouldn't take more than three hours, four tops," the tech said, missing John putting his finger over his mouth to keep quiet about moving to the front of the line.

"Front of the line?" Trip asked. The tech nodded, noticing John finally. John, with a wince on his face, wouldn't look at Trip. "Is all of this acceptable, Agent Fowler?" Trip asked. John was a bit surprised but ran with it.

"Sounds good to me," John answered. The tech left, and John began to study a picture in Trip's office, feeling four sets of eyes on him.

"Jessica, find out later what that's all about," Trip said. John spun around in time to see a grin on Jessica's face form. John shivered.

"That's got to be workforce harassment," John complained.

"I'm okay with that," Trip replied. John winced.

"Let's just say that I have a theory on the other case I'm working," John replied mysteriously. Trip paused and thought for a minute. He didn't want to hinder John by saying the wrong thing.

"Dr. Brian Nichols?" Trip asked. John nodded. "Where are you on that?"

"Nowhere, unless Captain Dodo here has something he'd like to share with the rest of the class," Jessica replied, staring at the back of John's head. John was looking at a spot on the wall, which just happened to be away from Jessica's gaze and Trip's look of annoyance.

"Fine, keep your secrets," Trip said. "If something happens, you'll tell us?" John nodded. Trip sighed. "So, what's our plan on our current serial killer suspect?"

"If we had some evidence that collaborated her story, would you be willing to listen to a crazy plan?" John asked.

"Just to make sure I understand, you're calling whatever plan you're cooking up crazy?" Ron asked. John nodded. Ron put his hand over his face. "Is anyone else scared when he admits up front that a plan is crazy?" Everyone except John nodded.

"What kind of evidence?" Trip asked.

"It will be ready in 4 hours or so," John answered. Trip looked at his watch.

"I hope to be home by then," Trip said, beginning to look more than a little peeved. John nodded and began to grin. Jessica groaned. Trip looked like he wanted to. Chet tried to hide the smile growing on his face, and Ron just sat back and watched like someone who slowed their car down to watch a car wreck.

"Why don't we hold her overnight to show her we're serious?" John asked. Trip couldn't believe what he was hearing.

"Why?" Trip asked. John acted confused. "What's the end game?"

"To see if we can get her to work with us," John replied.

"You think Liz did it," Jessica said, her arms crossed, playing back all the evidence in her head. "You think she helped her husband and Amanda is telling us the truth." John ignored his wife and stared at Trip. Trip looked at Jessica and then to John. Trip sighed.

"Give me some evidence in the morning, and we'll talk," Trip said, expecting a fight over not giving John a guarantee. John smiled, stood, and straightened his jacket. He started to leave, and then, against his better judgment, he turned to Jessica.

"I don't think Amanda is telling us the truth," John said directly to Jessica. Jessica looked a little surprised; John continued. "I know she's telling the truth," he said as he winked at her. He then turned and sauntered out of the room. Everyone just watched him go.

"I married him, why?" Jessica asked no one, staring at the open door.

"I have no idea," Trip said, wondering where his stomach pills were.

"Do you think he's wrong?" Ron asked. Jessica, Trip, and Chet all turned to look at him. "What?"

"No," Chet replied. "He's not wrong, but he doesn't have anything to back him up, and that's the problem. If whatever he's doing comes up with an answer other than what he wants, what is he going to do? What is John going to do if he can't clear Sam's daughter?" Ron turned to look out the door John just exited.

"You know, with what he went through, maybe he shouldn't be on this case," Ron began referring to John's PTSD episode. Jessica lightly laid her hand on his leg. Ron stopped and looked at her.

"Don't," she said, shaking her head. "He has to do this, because if he doesn't..." Jessica couldn't finish the sentence. She couldn't finish the sentence because if he didn't fix this, she wasn't for sure what he would do.

Chapter 59

Several hours later, John and Jessica were washing the dishes after dinner when they heard a knock on the door. John went to the door and was surprised by who he saw through the peephole.

"Madeline," he said as he opened the door. Jessica, looking surprised, came to the door. "Come in," John said as he stood out of the way so she could enter. Madeline came in and hugged Jessica. John shut the door and studied Madeline. Something was off, and John didn't know what. It was probably one of those personal things that he had trouble reading sometimes.

"What's wrong?" John asked softly. Jessica shot John a dirty look.

"Why do you assume something's wrong?" Jessica asked. Madeline smiled at John.

"I'm not assuming," John answered softly.

"Oh," Jessica answered, a little embarrassed. "Do you two need a minute?" she asked, pointing toward the bedroom where she could go hide.

"Nonsense, dear," Madeline said. "This is something both of you need to see," she said as she pulled what looked like a book out of her bag. "I've only kept two things from you in my life, John." John looked at the book and then at Madeline. "I kept your baby from you, and I kept Amanda from you."

"Are you pregnant?" John, confused as to where this was going, asked Jessica.

"What?" Jessica asked. "No, I don't think."

"What do you mean you don't think?" John asked. Madeline couldn't help but laugh at the two of them. Madeline laid her hand on John's shoulder to try and calm him.

"If she's pregnant, John, I know nothing about it," Madeline reassured him. "What I wanted to show you was this." Madeline handed John the book she had brought.

"It's a diary Sam kept. She told me she wanted me to keep this if anything ever happened to her. I think this is what she meant when she said it's time." John looked up at Madeline.

"When did she give you this?" John asked.

"A few days before she died," Madeline answered. "After you went," Madeline paused, not sure how to say what she wanted.

"On a drunken binge? Three sheets to the wind? Tied one on?" John offered.

"Yes," Madeline replied, shaking her head and smiling at John. "I took a look at the book and figured you weren't ready to deal with it after she died. In fact, I wasn't sure you would ever be ready to deal with it. I only give it to you now because we know that Amanda is Samantha's daughter." John looked down at the book. "I need to go."

"You can't stay?" Jessica asked. Madeline shook her head and smiled.

"I dragged Arthur into New York to see a play tonight, and that's exactly what I'm going to do," Madeline replied. The three said their goodbyes, and Madeline headed to the door. She stopped and turned back to John. "Can you help her?"

"I'm going to try, Madeline, for both of their sakes," John answered. Madeline patted John's face and left. Jessica and John stared at the book like it was a snake.

Chapter 60

"I guess we should open it," Jessica said, after several seconds of absolute quiet in the apartment. John nodded. He just stared at the book. Jessica studied him a second, nodded, and headed into the kitchen and came back with a cheesecake. She sat it on the table in front of the couch. She came back to John and guided him to the couch. As he sat down, he saw the cheesecake.

"When did you get cheesecake?" John asked incredulously.

"Your first wife's child is accused of murder," Jessica explained. "I figure that maybe having some comfort food around is a good call."

"Cheesecake is your comfort food," John replied as Jessica shoved a fork-full into his mouth. He chewed and nodded. "Although, right now, it was a pretty good idea."

"The freezer was too full, or I would have gotten cookie dough ice cream," Jessica said.

"Once again, your comfort food," John said. Jessica continued on, ignoring him.

"I've never asked you this before, but we've never been in this situation before," Jessica began. It was slowly dawning on John why she had comfort food.

"There's no alcohol in the house," John said. Jessica stared at him, amazed, again. "I mean, come on, if an alcoholic is going to lapse, what would be bigger than this?" Jessica nodded. She looked at John, a little unsure. John nodded for her to go ahead.

"What about the bottle that used to be in the freezer?" Jessica asked.

"You mean the one I used to look at every morning to remind me of my loss?" John asked. Jessica nodded. "The night after I talked at the AA meeting and we had coffee until who knows when in the morning, I poured it out when I got home." Jessica made a small sound that resembled a mouse squeaking. "Are you okay?" Jessica nodded, tears forming in her eyes. "What did I do?" John asked, panicking that he had messed up, but not knowing how.

"You poured it out when you got home after just talking with me?" Jessica asked. John nodded, still not sure what he had done and if it was good or bad. "Why?"

"Because you convinced me it was time to live my life," John answered. Jessica flung herself across the couch to hug him. "Easy! You'll spill the cheesecake!"

"I don't care," Jessica answered. John was okay with that. After all, it was just cheesecake, not pumpkin pie.

Chapter 61

Several hours later, John wandered into the living room, insomnia being his friend again. Tonight was different though. He couldn't stop from thinking about the diary. He sat down on the couch and stared at it on the table. He knew he needed to read it, but he really wasn't sure what good it would do.

"It's not going to read itself," John said to no one. He picked it up and opened the diary. He recognized Sam's handwriting immediately.

Dear Amanda,

I know I'm supposed to write Dear Diary, but this is for you. I know, I know, you're dead, but you still live on in my heart. Plus, I've met this therapist who was telling me about writing to their children sometimes helps parents deal with the heartbreak of losing them. I never got to know you, but for nine months, you were my little angel. I don't know what went wrong that day, but if it was anything I did, I am so sorry. I wanted so much to be your mommy.

I don't know who your daddy was. Well, not for sure. I have a feeling, but I don't think I could ever prove it, and it wouldn't do any good to fight that battle anyway. I met a man a few years later, and he is wonderful. Okay, he's a little different, but I know he would have loved you and been the best daddy in the world to you. His name is John. I'll tell you more about him later, but I think you two would get along great.

I just wanted you to know that after all these years, I still think about you, and I still miss you. I work with lots of little boys and girls now, and in some way, I hope that I can help them since I couldn't help you. You would have been eight today. I don't know what you would have wanted for your birthday, but I bought a little cupcake today and placed a candle on it. I sang happy birthday to you and blew out the candle. I hope you can forgive me for not taking proper care of you. I so wish we could have met. I bet we would have been the best of friends. I think you would have been just like me, and you would have been the best daughter ever! I love you, Amanda. Don't ever forget it!

Love,

Mommy

John closed the book and laid it on the table. Tears flowed from his face.

"Oh, Sam," he said softly, his cheeks streaked with tears. "She needs you so badly. I can't fix her, Sam. He's made her so twisted that she doesn't even seem to know up from down." Jessica walked out of the bedroom, saw John, and held him while he cried softly. She picked up the book, and began to read from it. John didn't want to hear anything else from it, so she to read it to herself. Sometimes, Jessica cried; sometimes, she laughed out loud; and, sometimes, she just shook her head at the loss. She closed the book, turned, and looked John right in the eye.

"She's more like me than I realized," John said, nearly in a whisper.

"What do you mean?" Jessica asked.

"She's broken just like me," John said, his eyes wandering toward the kitchen. Jessica knew he was looking where the bottle used to be in the freezer.

"Not broken, just bent," Jessica said softly. John looked at her, his eyes full of emotions. "You fix this, John," she said.

"How?" he asked. Jessica shook her head.

"You fix this, John Fowler," she said again, tears running down her face. "That's what Sam wanted in the graveyard. That's what she wanted at the Moores'. She said it wasn't her fault, so you FIX this!" Jessica fell into John, sobbing.

"I'll try the best I can," John answered. Jessica looked up at him, her face determined and tear-soaked.

John nodded. "I'll do it." Jessica nodded and snuggled up against John. "Sam, I need your help," he said softly. "Amanda needs your help." Silence answered him.

John sat and thought. He had one more idea, and it was one that was way out there. It was so far out in right field though that it might just work. He told Jessica about some of it. It shocked her, but she agreed. It might be just the thing. John sat and thought about the rest of the plan that was formulating in his head as they both sat there, watching the sun start to break on the horizon. John didn't like keeping Jessica in the dark, but it was all he had. He needed to keep her in the dark in case he was wrong about Elizabeth. As the sun began to peek through the blinds, Jessica wondered if their careers would ever be the same.

Chapter 62

The next morning, Trip walked into the foxhole, not knowing what to expect out of John. John was actively working two cases while his team was working another. Trip wondered if he should make John tell the team what was going on, but Trip didn't think so. This was personal. This was personal for Ron, Jessica, John, and even Chet. Trip took a deep breath and calmed himself. Nothing John did was going to surprise Trip this morning, Trip was sure of that. He didn't realize how wrong he could be.

As he walked in, he looked around for John and didn't see him. Ron and Chet were standing off to the side, looking uncomfortable. Jessica was leaning against the big desk in the middle of the room like she was waiting for Trip or someone. She looked very tired.

"Where's John?" Trip asked. Jessica took a deep breath, reached behind her, grabbed the book Madeline had given John last night, and handed it to Trip. Trip looked at it, confused. Jessica just nodded toward the book, Trip opened it, and began to read. He stopped after just a few seconds. His head snapped up toward Jessica. "Is this for real?"

"Madeline gave it to John last night," Jessica said. Trip went back to the book. He read the first letter that Sam had written to Amanda.

"Is it all like this?" he asked, struggling to keep the emotion out of his voice.

"Yeah," Jessica answered. "John's taking a personal day today, and won't be working for the FBI." Trip nodded and looked up at Jessica. There was an emotion running across her face he couldn't describe.

"You're about to tell me something that is going to blow my mind," Trip said, wondering if he was on the verge of a mental breakdown.

"Amanda is the Moores' granddaughter," Jessica began. She stopped, not sure how to go on.

"Oh, no," Trip whispered softly, really afraid of where this was going. Jessica, not knowing what to say, reached behind her, pulling out another paper, and handed it to Trip. Trip looked at it. It was a formal, printed letter, signed by John.

"He's recusing himself from the case?" Trip asked, shocked and confused all at once. "Why? He's never pulled himself off cases before, and he was closer to them then." Jessica looked at Chet. Chet and Ron looked as though they wanted to flee. "What can be worse?" Trip asked, scared to hear the answer.

"Apparently, John did more than just become a private investigator while he was away from the FBI," Jessica answered carefully. Trip stared at Jessica, completely confused. "Trip, as far as he's concerned, Sam would want him to treat her as his daughter." Jessica paused, fighting tears. "Trip, I agree with him," she blurted out and began to cry. Trip was beyond confused.

"He feels like he has to do whatever it takes to get her free," Chet said. Trip turned to look at him, still with no clue as to what was going on. "John doesn't want us in any trouble."

"With the law?" Trip asked. Chet tried to smile, and Ron just shook his head.

"Do you want me to tell him?" Ron asked. Chet shook his head and barreled ahead.

"It's funny you should mention law, Trip," Chet began. Trip stared at Chet in disbelief, not believing if what he was putting together in his head could possibly be true.

Chapter 63

"His bachelors, is it in criminal justice?" Trip asked. Well, demanded, more than asked. Chet nodded. Trip closed his eyes and admitted to himself he was wrong. John did surprise him today.

"How?" Trip asked in a choked voice.

"He did it on nights and weekends starting out," Jessica whispered. Trip's eyes popped open, and he stared at her. "He apparently asked then Senator Cosby to help him get in as a condition of him going undercover." Trip looked more confused than ever. "He apparently was already thinking about leaving the FBI and helping at-risk moms and their kids. It was something Sam wanted to do. It was one of the few things Sam ever kept from me. Sam apparently did write about it in the book. After Sam's death, John switched from part-time to full-time."

"You're telling me that John Fowler, while you were tailing him without his knowledge," Jessica turned a shade of red in embarrassment but never stopped Trip. "Was a licensed Private Investigator for the state of New York and went to law school? Not only that, while he was working undercover he went to law school, sometimes drunk out of his mind!"

"I knew he was taking some classes. I just thought it was to help him with the PI work," Jessica said softly. "Apparently, the mob boss Anthony Lucciano liked the idea of having his own lawyer as well, if John was to be kicked out of the FBI, which Anthony thought was possible given how they met." Trip looked ready to blow his top. He dreaded the next question, but it was the only thing that made sense in this mess.

"Did he pass the bar?" Trip asked through gritted teeth. Jessica couldn't answer. She only nodded. Trip felt his eyelid twitching. "I know it shouldn't be possible, but does he work for a law firm?" Trip just knew he couldn't.

Then, he looked at Jessica, who was staring at the floor. "You've got to be kidding me!"

"He called Arthur this morning about 5 a.m.," Jessica began. Trip had forgotten about the team mentioning Arthur. He had a bad feeling about what he was about to hear. "They talked, and apparently, Arthur had his law firm hire him on to work on one case and one case only."

"You're telling me John Fowler, Special Agent John Fowler with special congressional clearance from the United States Congress, is the legal representation for Amanda Nichols? And, to top it off, Arthur is paying him?" Trip looked ready to stroke out after that diatribe.

"No," Jessica said shaking her head. She didn't know whether to laugh or cry at the next part. Trip wasn't sure whether he could take anything else. "John's doing it pro bono." The chuckle that came from the far side of the room was contagious. The entire room had been so tense that the emotions broke like a dam. Laughter filled the room.

"If this was on TV or a movie, no one would believe it," Ron said through the laughter. Trip started toward the door.

"Trip, there's one more thing," Jessica said. Trip stopped in his tracks and began to chuckle as he turned. He looked back at three serious faces.

"You're not going to question her, are you?" Trip asked. They all shook their heads as one. "But, you want to watch in the observation room, don't you?" Trip asked with a twinkle in his eye. Trip could tell they were fighting to hold back the amusement on their faces. "Well, come on. I can't blame anyone for not wanting to miss this." With that, he turned and left with the other three scrambling behind him.

Chapter 64

Trip told the three to go ahead and go to the observation room. After they left him, he made a quick detour. When he showed up at the interrogation room a few minutes later, he had a folder in his hand. Jessica stood outside the door waiting for him.

"I wondered how long until you would want to talk," Trip said softly as he approached her.

"I didn't know, sir," Jessica said.

"I know, and that makes it worse," Trip said. Jessica looked a little confused.

"I think the question you and I have to find out from John is why," Trip explained. "If it was simply to become more familiar with the law so that he could run his PI business, then that's one thing." Trip paused, not sure if he should go forward with what he was thinking.

"Then why did he take the bar exam, and why get a JD? Why not get an EJD online or just not take the bar?" Jessica asked, and realized what Trip wasn't saying. "You think he was going to continue on with Sam's work?" Jessica really didn't think so, but she was hoping that was the answer.

"We've both known John a long time," Trip began carefully. "Do you see him doing that kind of work without Sam there?" Jessica wasn't for sure what Trip was asking. He sighed, smiled, and barged right ahead. "Do you think John has the personality to work with people like he would have to in those situations without Sam?" Jessica's eyes got wide as she thought about it.

"That would be a disaster," Jessica said, picturing a mother slapping John with her purse when John told her she was lying about something. She stared at Trip. "Why take the bar exam?"

"Well, the obvious answer is so he could practice law," Trip answered.

"Why would John want to practice law?" Jessica asked.

"To get someone on the stand to see if they were lying?" Trip asked. Jessica thought for a second. She shook her head at the thought that ran through her head. "What?"

"We know John," Jessica began, not liking what she was thinking but scared Trip was thinking the same thing. "We know he likes to see where the line is and push it for all it's worth."

"If not step right over it," Trip added. Jessica had to nod in agreement. Trip needed to get into the interrogation room so he came right out and said it. "Do you think he was looking for legal options and wanted to know what all he could legally get away with?" The look on Jessica's face told him that's exactly what she was thinking.

"There is another possibility," she added. Trip nodded.

"He was going to try and find a way to try Sam's killer?" Trip asked.

"He couldn't in criminal court," Jessica answered.

"But, he could in civil court," Trip replied. "If for some reason the killer got off in the criminal trial, he could sue." Jessica nodded, but that still didn't work in her mind. It was possible, but when factoring in John, she just didn't think it was probable.

"That doesn't answer why the bar," Jessica said. "That explains why the JD but not the bar."

"We have to ask him," Trip replied. Jessica nodded, jaw set. "Are we pulling punches on this one?"

"Nope," Jessica replied, beginning to look a little irritated. Trip prayed it was John she was irritated with and not him. Jessica handed him the book from earlier. "She needs to see this." Trip took it, nodded, and opened the door to the interrogation room as Jessica went to the observation room. As Trip stepped in, he suppressed a laugh at seeing John sitting right beside her. This was going to be fun.

Chapter 65

"Assistant Director Smothers," John said, nodding toward Trip as he walked in. Trip paused, not sure how to take that greeting. He decided to go along.

"Mr. Fowler," Trip responded. Amanda looked from John to Trip, confused.

"I thought you worked for him?" Amanda asked John.

"Not today," Trip answered.

"He's not in trouble is he?" Amanda asked.

"Not any more than usual," Trip replied. John touched her arm.

"As your legal counsel, I should inform you that I should be doing the talking for you," John said.

"How are you a lawyer and a FBI agent?" Amanda asked. Trip swore he heard muted laughter from the other room.

"Miss Nichols," Trip began trying to turn this into some sort of proper interview. "If this is Mr. Fowler's first case which I imagine it is, I can assure you, you are in as good of hands possible." John looked a little surprised. He gave Trip a small, tight smile and an acknowledging nod. "However," Trip went on, the smile fell from John's face. "You should know that I have no plans on prosecuting you and am releasing you."

"What?" John asked. Trip was sure he heard snickers this time.

"Mrs. Sapp has changed her statement," Trip said, trying to keep the smile off his face. However much he enjoyed seeing himself one up John, this was not the time or the place. "She has thought about what she saw, and she's not sure now what happened. There is not sufficient evidence to pursue the case against you, and quite frankly, it looks like what happened may have been self-defense." John looked conflicted. Trip knew that on one hand, John was happy that Amanda was about to go free, but now, it turned out he had recused himself from the case for no reason and made his work a little harder, not impossible, but harder. Trip appeared a little amused every time he glanced at John.

Trip pulled out Sam's book that Madeline had given John last night. "This appears to be yours," Trip said, pushing the book across the table to Amanda. "You might want to get the particulars from your lawyer, but it seems your mother wrote to you." Amanda stared at the book, then at Trip, not sure if she heard correctly. She shot John a look. Something started to form in her mind, and John didn't like what he was picking up. She turned to Trip.

"So, you're saying that my attorney over here did nothing for me," she said, pointing at John. Trip shook his head slightly.

"I wouldn't say nothing," John tried to interject. Amanda went on, ignoring him.

"And this book is written to me from my mother?" Amanda asked clarifying. Trip nodded. John was getting a bad feeling about how this was about to play out by looking at Amanda. He was trying to get Trip's attention. "So the woman that my attorney here claims never knew anything about me, wrote to me?" Trip looked a little surprised but nodded yes. Amanda put her hands around the book gently. Her face read of rage, but she treated the book like a prized possession.

"Amanda," John began. Amanda ignored him.

"Do you have anything else for me?" Amanda asked Trip. Trip shook his head no. "Tell him he's fired." With that, Amanda stood up, gave John a look of death, marched over to the door, opened it, and paused. She turned back to Trip.

"Please keep your agent away from me," Amanda said, venom dripping in her voice. "It shouldn't be hard now since I'm sure there's some sort of conflict of interest between being my lawyer and the agent assigned to my case."

"You did just fire me," John interjected. Amanda stared daggers at John.

"I thought I could trust you," Amanda said. John just sat there, not saying anything. She held up the book. "My mother wrote this book to me when she thought I was supposedly dead. You're just as bad as he was! You kept her away from me! I don't know if you didn't want me in your life, or you just wanted her all for yourself, but you kept us apart! You couldn't even see that I got this! I hate you!" With that, she stepped through the door and slammed it. Trip and John sat in uncomfortable silence for a few seconds.

"Well," John said straightening and buttoning his coat. "I think that went well." Trip stared at him like he was crazy.

Chapter 66

"We need to talk," Trip said, trying to find a way to break the uncomfortable silence.

"Do you want to chew me out here in front of the peanut gallery or in your office?" John asked. Trip looked at the glass, made a head gesture that seemed to say, "leave," and looked back at John.

"You know she's in the next room listening," John said. The door opened as he finished the sentence, and Jessica walked in, and sat down beside John. "Or, maybe she's not," John said, shrugging. He was staring at the floor like he was embarrassed.

"What's going on?" Trip asked.

"You mean about me getting my law degree and passing the bar, or do you mean representing Amanda?" John asked, and then his face lit up like he had an idea and leaned forward. "Or, if you're asking me about the problems in the world, I would like to choose that one to discuss, but I'm guessing that's not it." Neither Jessica nor Trip said anything. John appeared to be even more embarrassed.

"Why?" Jessica asked softly, putting her hand on his arm. John turned to her and gave her a sad smile.

"To not drink," John replied. Trip looked down at the table and then at Jessica. Her look met his. John didn't even notice. He had folded his hands in front of himself and was staring at them. He took a second and then began to speak softly.

"After Sam died, and we had our little episode here," he began and then paused. He looked around and saw the smile on Jessica's face. "Was it this room?" he asked her. She nodded. John nodded and continued. "I needed something to do. I was already going part time, and I opened the detective agency, but it was a joke. One evening Jeremiah came by." Trip and Jessica gave each other a surprised look. John grinned. "He came by to see if I had been drinking. You know Jeremiah. He wasn't going to pull any punches." John thought back to that time and shook his head.

"To say I was directionless was to put it nicely. I had been watching the proceedings on the mafia busts, but I still wasn't any closer to finding out who killed Sam." John looked away for a second. He turned back and looked toward his fists, never looking the two of them in the eye. "Jeremiah put the idea in my head that it would be something if I could be the one who prosecuted whoever killed Sam. The way I could read people…it would be a huge advantage with a jury, and I could really get to a witness, but of course, that wasn't possible since I hadn't gotten my JD or passed the bar exam. That's all he said, but I took it and ran with it. He used me against myself." John paused and sat quietly for a minute.

"He gave you a reason to live and not to drink," Jessica said softly. John shook his head, a tear falling down his face onto his arm.

"Not to live," John replied. "Just not to die. That would be the better way to put it."

Chapter 67

"I've never told anyone how close I came to ending it all," John said, his voice cracking with emotion. "I never told anyone how hopeless it all seemed. How do you explain to people that she was the only person who really saw me for me? How do I explain that she accepted the screwed up mess that I was? How do I explain that for all my faults, I was the person she loved?" John turned toward Jessica. "The only other person I even trusted like that, I told her I hated her." Jessica closed her eyes trying to fight back tears. Trip looked away, misty eyed. John barked a laugh.

"I don't know if you noticed, but I'm not the easiest person to get along with," John said. Trip and Jessica both chuckled. "Sam taught me I should never apologize for being me, but without her around, it was just so hard. So, I poured my everything into the program, the agency, and then the bar. It was after I passed the bar that it dawned on me that the District Attorney would never let me prosecute the case, much less hire me. By that time, I had started to heal, not much, but enough to know I didn't want to die. I didn't know that I wanted to live yet, but I didn't want to die."

"John," Jessica began softy but couldn't finish the sentence. He patted her hand, and she looked at him with hurt in her eyes.

"I had been going to meetings for a while, so the alcoholism was under control to the best of my ability, and listening to some of those poor messed up souls made me realize that maybe, one day, I could get my life back together. At least, I could get even with whoever took out Sam before I took the big sleep."

Trip stared at John for a second.

"Are you telling me after you solved Sam's case, you planned on killing yourself?" Trip asked. John didn't say anything for a second.

"The best answer I can give you is I wasn't going to do anything to get myself killed before I figured it out," John answered. "That was before Chet barged into my apartment and brought me back into the fold." John looked over at Jessica and took her hand. He squeezed it and gave her a smile. "Then, I had other reasons to live." John looked at the mirror. "That includes you, too." John waited for a minute, and then, the door opened, and Chet walked in, red-eyed. Ron was behind him, looking very unsure.

"Come on in, Ron," John said. "You're family now." Ron came in, looking a little uncomfortable.

"If I hadn't," Chet began, not able to finish the sentence.

"You did," John replied. "You did, and I figured out that I wanted to have a life again." John turned to Trip. "I hope you understand why I didn't really want to talk about the lawyer thing." Trip nodded.

"Why recuse yourself of the case and represent her though?" Trip asked. "You had to know the case was flimsy." John grinned. Trip wanted to groan. Why did he have that stupid grin?

"Of course I did," John answered. Trip closed his eyes.

"You planned this?" Trip asked.

"Not all," John replied. "But, like I said, it went well."

Chapter 68

"I am totally lost," Trip said.

"You and me both," Jessica added. "And I was there for more of it than you were."

"Are you all ready to accept something is not right about Kenneth Nichols?" John asked.

"I think I can go that far," Trip admitted. Everyone in the room agreed.

"Can you accept that if my theory is right, it would place Amanda in danger if Kenneth thought I was close to her?" John asked. Trip thought for a second.

"If your theory is right, then yes," Trip finally agreed. Once again, the group agreed.

"Then, do you see what I just did?" John asked, a twinkle in his eyes and his grin growing. Jessica groaned.

"You just made Trip write into the official report what happened," Jessica said. Trip was confused. "You just saw Amanda fire John as her lawyer and accuse him of keeping Amanda and Sam apart. You effectively have just told Kenneth that while Amanda may not trust him, she sure doesn't trust John." John nodded.

"You set me up!" Trip said, his mouth open from shock. John shrugged.

"I needed it to not look staged," John replied.

"Wait," Ron interjected. "What are you talking about?"

"John thinks that someone above me, or around me, is getting information to Kenneth," Trip answered. He looked directly at John and continued. "Frankly, I think he's right."

"There's not a lot of people above you," Ron said. Trip nodded.

"There are probably more people that see Trip's reports than we realize, Ron," John said. "If we're right, Kenneth will back off Amanda."

"He's still going to be upset with her," Trip countered.

"I bought her some time," John replied.

"The biggest problem you have now is why did Mrs. Sapp change her statement," Jessica said. John didn't say anything.

"I don't know," Trip said, "But I can't talk to you about it." This time, John looked shocked.

"You're not going to," John began but trailed off, seeing the smile on Trip's face.

"Oh, you better believe I am," Trip replied. "We're doing this one completely by the book."

"You would say that," John muttered. Trip looked at John sharply, and John looked embarrassed. "Trip, I had no right to say that. I'm sorry." Trip smiled.

"I have a certain image to maintain in this agency," he replied. John stared at Trip, and a smile began to grow on both men's faces.

"You certainly do," John replied. He slapped the table. "I guess you three have some paperwork and follow up on the Sapp case. You know, that stuff that I hate to do? I have to go to work on murder of Dr. Nichols and another case I've been looking at." Trip nodded, smiling.

"What are you two up to?" Jessica said.

"We're not up to anything," John replied. "We're just doing this investigation by the book." Trip nodded.

"Completely by the book," Trip replied. With that, both men got up and left the room, smiling.

"I don't believe what I just saw," Jessica said. "They're in cahoots!"

"Nope," Ron said, grinning. "They're just doing things by the book." Jessica groaned.

"Not you, too?" she asked. Ron nodded and paused, the smile leaving his face.

"I guess that means he can't help me with my murder cases," Ron said sadly.

"Don't be too sure about that," Chet said. Jessica nodded. "Jessica's right. They're in cahoots, and when those two are up to something…" Chet trailed off.

"What?" Ron said, curious. Chet shrugged.

"I have no idea; they've never been in cahoots before!" Chet admitted.

Chapter 69

Amanda stormed out of the FBI building. She couldn't believe she had trusted him! John used her just like her father had. Didn't anyone want her? Didn't anyone want her for what she was? She looked down at the book she was carrying and began to think that there might be someone, but she was dead. A hand touched her shoulder, and she jumped. She turned around, ready to lash out but paused when she saw who it was.

"Are you okay?" Liz Sapp asked. Amanda wasn't sure how to react. Because of her, she had spent the night in jail, but she might have also saved her life. "I want to apologize. With everything that happened... I don't know what happened that night. All I know is men have hurt me my entire life, and I don't know how to-" she stopped because a homeless man stumbled into her. "Watch it!" Both ladies covered their faces. The smell of the man was horrible. The man had crashed into her and was tangled up with her. She was trying to push him off and cover her nose at the same time.

"Sorry," he slurred. He tipped his cap at her and stumbled along the street.

"Are you okay?" Amanda asked. Liz was brushing her clothes off, trying to get the grime and the smell off her. She gave Amanda a grateful look.

"I'm okay," Liz said with a soft smile. "Do you want to get some coffee?"

"I think I'd like that," Amanda replied. "What were you saying about men using you?"

"I'll tell you all about it in a few," Liz responded. "Let's go find someplace to have a drink." The two women headed down the street. As they passed an open alley, they saw the homeless man, or maybe it was another one-they all looked alike to Liz-sitting against the wall. "I do feel sorry for the poor men, but surely there is something that can be done about them."

The ladies walked a few blocks until they found a small coffee place that wasn't one of those chain places. They placed their order and had a seat.

"As I was saying," Liz continued from their earlier discussion. "Men have hurt me my entire life, and I have become tired of it." Amanda looked at her, not sure where this was going.

"What have they done to you?" Amanda asked.

"Used me as an end to a means," Liz responded. "I'm not a man-hater. Don't get me wrong. I am just tired of these power hungry men using us to get what they want. My ex-husband was a terrible person. He made me kill people, Amanda. At first, he had me shoot them after he killed them, but eventually, I had to kill them before he could stab them." Amanda looked down at her coffee and then at Liz.

"What happened in that parking garage?" Amanda asked. Liz gave her a sad smile.

"Our lives changed forever," Liz answered.

Chapter 70

Liz looked down at her coffee and thought back to two nights prior. She had found Dwayne talking to Amanda. At first, Liz had thought Amanda was some floozy that he had picked up until she realized Dwayne was going to kill her. That was the last straw. She could understand if he wanted to have an affair with Amanda. She was very attractive. She could forgive that. After all, Dwayne was a man, and all men were weak when it came to their physical urges. But, killing someone else without her? That was a betrayal that could not, and would not, be forgiven.

A few times in the bar, Dwayne had looked in her direction, but her new disguise had been good enough to fool him. She had followed the two of them to the parking garage, and she had figured exactly when he was going to kill Amanda.

Dwayne had his arm around Amanda's neck when Liz had stepped out from behind the car she was hiding. When she aimed the gun, Amanda had enough sense about her to stomp on Dwayne's foot. Dwayne had let go of Amanda in surprise. Amanda started to run, when Dwayne collected himself enough to bring the knife handle down on the back of Amanda's skull to make her woozy.

Amanda almost crashed to her knees but managed to stay upright. She turned, and with all the strength she had, she brought her knee up into Dwayne's groin. She proceeded to collapse. Liz quickly came up behind Dwayne and stuck a needle full of etorphine that she got from her veterinarian friend long ago in his neck. Well, he had been a friend until she killed him. She had always been careful with the medicine since it was extremely powerful. She had only used it a few times before she met Dwayne. It was always good to have a few secrets in any marriage.

After Dwayne hit the ground, unconscious, Liz knew she had to cover her tracks, and what better way than to set up someone else for the kills. She carefully took the knife out of Dwayne's hand. She drug Amanda over to Dwayne, positioned herself behind Amanda, took Amanda's hands, and gripped them on the knife. She looked down at her husband and smiled as she used Amanda's hands to drive the knife through her husband's heart. He died quite quickly.

All of these thoughts flashed through Liz's mind in just a few seconds. She looked up from her coffee to Amanda.

"I had to get back control," Liz began cautiously. "I had had enough."

"You killed him?" Amanda asked. Liz nodded slightly.

"I'm sorry I framed you," Liz said, looking down at her coffee, seemingly ashamed. "I thought you were his new girl and were about to join him in his mad crusade." Amanda laughed.

"You don't understand," Amanda said. "I was having to fight off a bunch of men at a club, and he offered to join me, to just talk." Liz gave her a tight smile.

"That's what he does," she replied softly. Amanda's mouth dropped open.

"You mean, he was going to kill me?" Amanda asked. Liz nodded.

"What did you think happened?" Liz asked. Amanda shook her head.

"I really don't remember," she admitted. "He knocked me a little silly. I think he had his arm around my throat, but I thought maybe he was trying to protect me." Liz nodded.

"The brain tries to protect us," Liz replied. "It gives us scenarios that make sense and does the least amount of damage to our psyche."

"Are you a psychologist?" Amanda asked. Liz shook her head.

"Just lots of therapy," Liz replied. Amanda smiled. "Do you think we can be friends?" Amanda nodded.

"I'm glad to find someone who understands what I'm going through," Amanda replied. Liz smiled. Amanda thought the smile was full of warmth, but it wasn't. The smile was cold and calculating, just like Liz. She had a new plan. Since men were too unpredictable, she needed a new partner, and this one had been hand delivered to her. She couldn't believe her luck.

Chapter 71

"Does anyone know what etorphine is?" Ron asked. John rolled his chair to the door of his office and stuck his head out like a prairie dog popping his head out of his hole.

"The medicine used by veterinarians?" John asked. Chet gave John a weird look and began to look it up on the internet. Jessica was more than a little surprised as well and got up from her desk and came to the door. Chet was looking at his monitor in surprise. John was smiling and nodding, knowing he was right. Chet looked at Jessica, shrugged, and nodded to Ron. John clapped his hands.

"Find it in the victim, Ron?" John asked. Ron nodded. John had a smirk on his face and was nodding.

"Well, isn't that interesting," John said. "Did Liz ever admit to being involved with the other murders?" Ron closed the folder, crossed his arms, and stared at John.

"Yeah," Ron replied. "They didn't bring charges because they thought she was coerced." John nodded, rolled back to his computer, stopped, rolled back to the door, shut it, rolled back to the desk, picked up the phone, and made a phone call.

Jessica squinted her eyes and watched John. He had done strange things before, but this was a whole new level of strange. John had received at least ten phone calls in the past two hours. On top of that, there had been numerous texts, at least twenty files brought to him, and to complete the strangeness, he was using his computer. By himself. With no help. Now, that was odd.

John got up from his chair, shut down his computer, started out the door, stopped, went back, grabbed the files that had been brought to him, locked them in a drawer and headed out of his small office into the foxhole.

"You're locking up files?" Jessica asked as he walked by. John paused and looked at Jessica. Chet turned when he heard Jessica. Ron lifted his head and looked at John and Jessica. Chet started toward John.

"What's going on, boss?" Chet asked.

"Just a case I'm working on," John replied, turning his head toward Chet.

"Does it have anything to do with our case?" Jessica asked. John turned slowly toward her.

"It has nothing to do with Dwayne," he replied.

"The murder in D.C.?" she countered.

"Not directly," John responded. Chet and Ron exchanged looks, and then, both turned toward Jessica. Jessica had been leaning against the door frame up until this point. She now straightened and crossed her arms in front of her.

"What is going on, John?" Jessica asked. John looked around the room and wondered how he was keeping everyone out of this one.

Chapter 72

"Give me the rest of the day, and I'll tell you everything tonight," John said to the three that were staring at him.

"Boss," Chet began. John held up his hand.

"Listen, I have to be somewhere, now," John said urgently. Jessica gave a side head nod toward the door, and John took off. "I'll text you all the time and place later. I promise." And, with that, he was gone.

"We've missed something," Jessica said. "Pull the board back up Ron." Ron went to his computer. Chet went to his computer and began typing furiously. "What are you working on, Chet?" Chet smiled, hit a button, and a map with a flashing icon appeared on a small section of the big screen.

"After his last run in with Bruce, I tagged his cell phone," Chet replied.

"Chet, that's devious," Jessica chided. "I like it." Ron was typing something on his computer, and the map that showed Dwayne's kills popped up on the screen. All three looked up at the screen and began to drift to the middle of the room. They found themselves standing side by side, trying to figure out what it was John saw that they didn't.

"I don't get it," Chet said. "There's Dwayne's first kill, and it follows the pattern until he marries Liz, and she joins him in-"

"That's it!" Jessica and Ron said as one. They turned and looked at each other in surprise.

"I don't get it," Chet replied. Ron ran over to the files, found what he was looking for, and brought it back to the group. He pointed to the cause of death. Jessica glanced at it, made a face, looked at Ron, and shook her head ruefully.

"It was right in front of our faces," Jessica said.

"I was so concentrated on the knife killings that I missed it," Ron replied.

"Missed what?" Chet asked exasperated. Jessica turned and headed to her office. Ron took the file and showed Chet.

"This was the first kill using the knife and gun," Ron explained.

"Cause of death is by gunshot," Chet replied, not getting it.

"The first murder she was forced to be a part of, she killed her victim with a shot to the brain. A perfect shot?" A look of understanding slowly crawled across Chet's face. Jessica came out of her office with a knife. How she had gotten it into the building Ron wasn't sure, but she was heading toward John's desk.

"What are you doing?" Ron asked. Chet turned and looked. He chuckled.

"She's prying his desk open," Chet replied like he had seen her do it numerous times.

"Should she?" Ron asked.

"You want to tell her not to?" Chet countered. Ron started to respond but thought better of it.

Chapter 73

Jessica fiddled with the lock for about ten seconds before the drawer popped opened. She pulled out the files and brought them over to the big table.

"There's over twenty files here," Chet said.

"And, all of the victims are male, killed with a gunshot to the head," Ron said, flipping through files. Jessica scanned several files, putting each one she looked at in two separate piles. She paused on one. She read it for a second and slapped the file on her leg in frustration.

"He's got her," she muttered.

"Who has gotten what?" Chet asked.

"John," Jessica replied, staring at the map on the big screen. She was irritated. That was the only word to describe her. The three of them had worked so hard, but he had figured it all out. He hadn't done anything wrong or dirty. He had just worked the case from another angle.

"He thought from the beginning, there might be a second killer," Jessica said softly to Ron. Ron paused, thought about what she said, and nodded in agreement.

"But, he didn't know?" Chet asked.

"I don't think so," Jessica replied, slowly walking toward the big screen. "I think he thought there was a second killer." Jessica pointed at the spot where the victim was killed with the stabbing only in New York. "He kept going back to this spot."

"Which is the first kill after the circle was broken in New York," Ron said, pointing toward the half circle around New York. Jessica turned to Ron, nodding begrudgingly. She handed the file in her hand to Ron who looked at it. He read for a second, closed his eyes, and groaned.

"What?" Chet asked exasperated.

"Veterinarian, shot in the head," Ron replied. "Except this time there was a robbery. Etorphine was stolen."

"Wasn't that found in Dwayne?" Chet asked. Ron and Jessica both nodded.

"He linked it all together," Chet said in wonderment.

"He kinda cheated," Jessica said, still irritated.

"He took a risk," Ron said. "He let us work the sure thing and took the hunch." Jessica turned to Ron.

"I swear his hunches," she began but quit and just shook her head.

"So, how does this tie in with what happened in D.C.?" Chet asked. Jessica's eyes opened in surprise to the question.

"I don't know," she admitted.

"He's using her as bait," Ron said, going back to the computer and typing. Pictures of all the victims came up. Ron looked at Jessica. "You said to him, 'You're playing a dangerous game, Agent Fowler,'" Ron reminded her. Jessica shook her head.

"I had no idea," she responded. "He'd never do that. He'd never leave Amanda alone with Elizabeth, not if he thought this about her."

"What if someone was watching?" Chet asked. Jessica looked perplexed.

"Who?" Jessica asked. "Who outside of this room would he find to do it?"

Coffee Shop
Amanda and Liz

Chapter 74

Amanda exited the coffee shop and looked across the street. For a second, she was surprised. She swore she saw John Fowler in the alley across from the coffee shop. A bus moved slowly through traffic, blocking off her view from the alley, and when it passed, all she saw was a homeless man and a trash dumpster. Amanda was fairly sure the homeless man had been there before, and unless John had dived into a dumpster, which Amanda was sure he wouldn't, the vision had been a figment of her imagination.

"I'll see you later tonight?" Elizabeth asked Amanda, breaking her from her thoughts.

"Of course," Amanda answered, wondering why she thought she was seeing John.

"I'll text you and set it up later," Elizabeth said and left. Amanda considered going to the alley for just a second but knew she had to be seeing things. There was no way John would tail her, and even if he had, he wouldn't dive into a dumpster just to hide from her. Amanda shook her head and headed the opposite direction of Elizabeth.

From across the street, what looked to be a homeless man watched them go their separate ways. When both were out of sight, he got up quickly and went to the side of the huge garbage bin that had a door opened opposite of the coffee shop. The man pulled the plastic door back, and there sat John.

"Are you okay?" Hank asked.

"Peachy," John answered.

"I've never seen anyone as dedicated as you when it comes to hiding from the person he's tailing," Hank said.

"Thanks," John said, pulling a banana peel off his suit and tossing it in the bin.

"When I said hide behind the garbage bin, I meant behind it, not actually dive in," Hank said. John just stared at him. "And, you pulled the door shut. That's dedication." John continued to stare at Hank.

"Don't ever tell my wife about this," John answered. Hank smiled.

"She'll probably figure it out by the smell," Hank replied. Hank pulled his phone out, and there were two blips on the map that came up on his screen. He held his hand out, and John handed Hank his phone. Hank messed with it for a second, and handed it back to John. John stared at it.

"The blue dot is Amanda?" John asked. Hank nodded. "And, the red is Elizabeth?" Hank nodded again and held his hand out. John took it as Hank helped John out of the large bin. When he got on the ground, he looked at his suit. It was probably ruined, but it was worth it. He knew exactly where both women were at any given time.

Chapter 75

"The tracking device you slipped in the book was genius," Hank said. John smiled. He had decided early that morning that both women needed to be tracked. He knew that Amanda would take the book, and if it didn't come from him, she would never suspect a thing. While Jessica was in the shower, John had called Hank and told him the plan. John had met Hank, had gotten the chip implanted in the book, and had given the book back to Jessica while he took care of another part of the plan. Then, Jessica gave it to Trip, and Trip gave it to Amanda without a clue of the tracking device.

John's favorite part of the plan was when Hank, in full homeless bum outfit, bumped into Elizabeth and attached the tracking device in her purse. It was tiny but powerful. It was inside a pen, and John was pretty sure Elizabeth used the purse to carry her gun. He felt safe that Elizabeth would keep her gun on her at all times.

"I think you should know that you might get credit in clearing over twenty murders by the time this is over," John told Hank. A smile about split Hank's face in two. "If we get really lucky, there's another fifteen or more we can get her on with Dwayne."

"She's bad news," Hank said. John nodded.

"The worst," John admitted. "You'll stay on Amanda?" Hank nodded.

"If the two get together, you need to let me know immediately," John said. He sighed. "I've got to get home and change. I have to tell everyone what's going on."

"If you can get her to turn in the evidence on her dad, can you bust him?" Hank asked. John nodded.

"I can get him and two others," John replied, a grin on his face. Hank smiled.

"You should probably go shower," Hank said. John nodded, shook hands with Hank, and took off. He hailed a cab. It took several attempts because the first couple pulled away when John opened the door, and the cab drivers got a smell of him.

When John got home, he took the suit and put it in a garbage bag with the intent of burning it. After a long hot shower and then a second one because he kept getting lingering whiffs of something dying, John began texting people with the meeting time and location. John knew they would be upset with him, but this case was on the edge of closing.

John didn't like using Amanda like this. He was afraid she would never forgive him. He had gotten her cleared; that had been part of the plan. What he hadn't counted on was the friendship she had seemed to strike up with Elizabeth. John had thought in a day or two, after he closed the murders Elizabeth was involved in and proved to Amanda that he knew she was the president's daughter, he could smooth things over with her. Now...now, he wasn't sure what to do. Somehow, he had to make things right with her, and he wasn't good at that.

Chapter 76

While John was in thought about how to make things right with Amanda, the door opened, and Jessica entered the apartment. She saw John and smiled. The smile quickly fell from her face.

"What died in here?" she asked with a look of disgust on her face.

"Oh, that's what I've been smelling," John replied. "I spent some time in a dumpster today and forgot about my suit over there in the garbage bag." Jessica stared at John.

"Seriously," she began. "Did the village call about getting their idiot back?" John gave her a look as she walked over, grabbed the bag, held it at arm's length, walked it out of the apartment, and dropped it in the trash chute. She came back in, looked at John, and shook her head. "Do I even want to know how you ended up in a dumpster?"

"Probably," John admitted. "But I have a much bigger problem right now."

"I'm all ears," Jessica said.

"My plan hasn't gone exactly how I wanted it to," John admitted.

"And?" Jessica asked. John stared at her, confused. Jessica chuckled and went into the bedroom to get ready. "I mean, when has one of your plans ever gone exactly right?"

"What does that mean?" John asked, sitting on the arm of the sofa facing the bedroom as he talked.

"Oh, don't act all shocked and surprised," Jessica responded. It sounded like she was in her closet. John wondered if he should go in and help her. He decided not to. He might get distracted and he needed all his brain power right now to figure this problem with Amanda.

"Give me one example," John said.

"Knoxville, shootout with Bruce, the Archibald takedown," Jessica began.

"I wasn't officially there for Archibald," John retorted.

"You weren't supposed to be there at all," Jessica replied. "That's my point, John. You do much better on the fly than you do with a plan. Remember, I only agreed to marry you after you abandoned the speech you prepared and just told me how you felt."

"Don't remind me," John said. "The whole thing still gives me a headache." Jessica stuck her head out of the bedroom and gave him a smile. John couldn't help himself and smiled back. "Need any help?"

"Nope," she replied, coming out of the bedroom already changed. John gave a low whistle. "Flattery will get you everywhere." John started toward her. "Down boy. We have somewhere to be."

"Your loss," John said and offered her his arm. She took it, and they headed out the door to the meeting of the minds.

Chapter 77

Jessica and John entered a little bar she had never seen before.

"Are you sure we should be here?" Jessica asked.

"Sure," John replied. "Why shouldn't we?"

"You do remember you have a drinking problem?" Jessica asked.

"I don't have a drinking problem," John replied with a smile. "I have a problem stopping." Jessica wasn't smiling. "Too soon?" Jessica just stared at him. "Too soon," he said. John continued to walk to the back as Jessica just stared at him, wondering if he even realized some of the things he said sometimes. That was probably why she missed all the men in suits and earpieces that wanted to pat her down. John put a hand on her shoulder before she attacked anyone.

"They're Secret Service," John said. Jessica looked at him and then at the corner booth. She smiled as she saw Jeremiah and Trip.

"Please don't hurt these boys, Jessica ma' dear," Jeremiah said with a smile on his face. "It's hard to find good help."

"Are you sure this is a good idea, John?" Trip asked. "You do have a drinking problem."

"Really?" John asked. Jessica shot him a look. "Apparently, no one finds me funny." John sat down, and Jessica joined him. Jeremiah watched John as John watched Jeremiah.

"I guess it's time to come clean," Jeremiah said. John shrugged.

"Not necessarily," John replied. "But, if you do, I need you to wait for our other two guests." Jeremiah nodded, deep in thought.

"I would think this place would be a bit more crowded," Jessica said.

"It's usually packed," John replied. "But, the owner is a friend, and I was told they make a killer Cuban sandwich here. I hope you don't mind?" Jessica smiled at him and then thought more about what he said.

"What kind of favor?" she asked.

"Well, she hired me to catch her husband," John replied and looked around the room. "As a result, when it came time for her divorce…" John trailed off and glanced around the room. "So, whenever I want to throw a party, I have my own private room where no alcohol will be served."

"And, that's why you chose to come here," Trip said, finishing the story for him. John shrugged. Chet and Ron came into the room, and the conversation shifted. They were seated, menus were brought, and everyone ate for a while.

"We know," Chet said, trying to sound cryptic.

"Told you they'd eventually figure it out," John said to Trip.

"What?" Chet said. Trip just smiled.

"Oh, come one. How more obvious did I have to act?" John said. He turned to Jessica. "Did you pry the lock open?" Jessica stopped eating mid-bite and looked at John. Jeremiah roared with laughter.

"You're enjoying this," Chet accused. John nodded.

"Tell me what you know, and I'll fill in the rest," John said.

Chapter 78

"Long story, short, you suspect Liz of helping Dwayne all these years," Chet began. "You also believe she killed before she met him, and you've put it all together. I'm guessing that chemical that Ron mentioned helped your case." John nodded. "So where does Amanda fit in?" John looked down at the table. A sad smile covered his face.

"She actually got caught in the middle of something she had nothing to do with," John replied. "I was talking to her about the death of her grandfather --"

"Alleged," Trip interrupted. John grinned. Trip closed his eyes. Ron shook his head, and Jessica dropped her fork and looked at him.

"That look means you know, and you have proof," Jessica said. John nodded as the grin grew. "You didn't tell me?" John shrugged.

"I may have neglected to tell you several things along the way," John admitted. Jeremiah was chuckling.

"You do keep things interesting, ma' boy," Jeremiah said.

"I had the lab compare DNA between Amanda and Dr. Nichols," John said. Jessica made a face, jerked her head forward angrily, and brought her fist down on the table, making a few plates jump.

"I should have thought of that," she said under her breath. The whole table heard her and didn't make eye contact.

"That's what that lab tech meant in my office," Trip said. John nodded.

"Okay, then why didn't her DNA match her father's?" Chet asked.

"Who says it doesn't?" John responded. Everyone gave John a strange look except for Jeremiah and Trip.

"The database," Chet replied.

"Maybe the database is wrong," John replied.

"How is that even possible?" Jessica asked. She stared at John. She happened to see Jeremiah's face. She quickly scanned the table and noticed the look on Trip's face as well. "Okay, this has hit a whole new level of John weird." John shrugged.

"I'm just throwing out a hypothesis," John replied. Jessica shook her head.

"Don't give me that," Jessica replied. "Right before you were shot, we stumbled onto some things at the Moores' home, and Jeremiah and Trip sat there, looking the same way they do now. You two know something, and John has figured it out. There's something he won't tell me that he believes isn't his to tell. I know it's not you he's worried about," pointing toward Trip. "So, it has to be you," she said pointing at Jeremiah.

"Boy, don't let anyone ever tell you that you marry women that don't have the bravery of an amorous porcupine during mating season," Jeremiah said. John tried to work that one out in his head but came up with nothing. "I guess I have something I have to share with you." Jeremiah looked up at his Secret Service agents. "Don't let anyone in here until I give the okay." The men nodded. Jeremiah looked around the table and sighed.

"Would you like me to?" John asked. Jeremiah nodded.

"I would be much obliged," Jeremiah said. John nodded and looked around.

"Remember that saying that when you take away the impossible, whatever left, no matter how unlikely, is the truth?" John asked. Everyone nodded. "Keep that in mind as I tell you this one."

Chapter 79

"What if I told you that Kenneth Nichols had a double?" John began. "Would that surprise any of you?" Jeremiah looked at John strangely. John looked around, and everyone nodded.

"A lookalike to be seen someplace to throw off any would be assassins," Chet said. "That makes sense."

"What would it take to make him look exactly the same?" John asked Chet. Chet thought.

"If they were close, you could fool a lot of people with some surgery," Chet replied. "Are you saying the president had a double?"

"We know that Dr. Nichols and Amanda are grandfather and granddaughter by DNA, so why doesn't the DNA match Kenneth?" John asked. Chet thought for a minute.

"The DNA on file is not a familial match to his father and daughter," Chet said, talking it through. "That means the DNA on file doesn't belong to Kenneth Nichols. As crazy as that sounds, there are actual national security reasons as to why it wouldn't be."

"No," Ron interjected. "The DNA file we're talking about is used to make sure someone is the president. You're saying that the president circumvented the system."

"No, the evidence is saying that," John replied. Trip was looking at John. John flashed him a quick smile when no one was watching. Jeremiah looked ready to cry. He couldn't believe what John was doing. John was telling them everything while protecting Jeremiah at the same time.

"There has to be more to this," Chet began. John shook his head.

"They're may be, but what does it matter?" John said. "We're out to solve this murder, and that's it." Trip nodded.

"He could be protecting himself from Amanda," Jessica said. Everyone looked at her. "Think about it, if she said he was her father, and given what we know about how she was conceived, it would be a scandal, not to mention the criminal charges that would be brought against him."

"None of this proves murder," Trip said. John looked at him and nodded.

"But, it does get us one step closer as to proving that Kenneth Nichols is not the standup guy everyone thinks he is," John said. "We go where the evidence leads us. And, right now, its saying that Kenneth Nichols has done something to his DNA file. Can I bust him yet? No. Am I starting to build a case? Oh, yeah!" Jeremiah gave John a small smile and shook his head. He mouthed, "Thank You" to John when no one was looking. John gave him a small head nod.

"Okay, but what does this have to do with Amanda and Liz Sapp?" Chet asked.

"It proves that Amanda wasn't lying about Kenneth, and I don't think she lied about Dwayne. I know she didn't kill Dwayne," John replied.

"You would have had a hard time proving all of that," Jessica said, giving John a glance as she took a sip of her drink. "I mean, if Liz hadn't retracted her earlier statement, Amanda would have gone to jail, regardless of your lawyer skills." John began to grin. Jessica sat the glass down and stared at him. "You can't tell me you're taking credit for her changing her story." The grin changed to a smile.

"I just give credit where credit is due," John replied. Jessica gave him a look and a nod that seemed to say, "That's what I thought."

"Of course, I am due all the credit."

Chapter 80

"How can you possibly think that?" Jessica growled.

"I guess this is where I lay all of my cards on the table," John said, feeling the stares and glares from his friends. He turned to Jessica. "You remember that morning I went in early?" Jessica nodded.

"You told me that you had a law degree that evening, or morning, or whenever it was, and you were going to represent Amanda. You told me you had to make sure that she got out of the system as fast as possible before her father decided she was turning over evidence on him." Jessica watched John as she talked. He nodded when she was through but gave no other indications of anything else.

"That much is all correct," John replied. "It was when you went to the shower that the rest of my plan went into action." Jessica closed her eyes for a second. "You okay?"

"Just saying a prayer to give me the strength not to murder you," Jessica said.

"I say the same one daily," Trip added. John made a mocking laugh face at him.

"You all remember Hank?" John asked. "Hank was the undercover cop that helped us at Dwayne's murder scene. I asked Hank to don his undercover clothes and follow Liz. He had a better idea that I'll explain later. Hank had already given me a transmitter to follow someone, so I slipped it into Sam's diary."

"You do play with fire, John Fowler," Jessica said softly. John shrugged.

"You haven't heard anything yet," John replied. "I went in to the office before anyone else. I went to the holding room and told Liz that I didn't think that we'd find her guilty of her husband's murder. I went on to say that when all the evidence came back, it wouldn't look good for Amanda. I told Liz the way Amanda's father used her all those years, the way she trusted no one, and how the story she told had no evidence to back it up."

"You played her and me!" Trip exclaimed.

"What do you mean played you, Trip?" Chet asked.

"John knew that Trip would end up questioning Amanda," Ron answered. Trip nodded. "John also knew that Trip would check in on the only witness to the death, and when she changed her story…" Ron trailed off, smiling and held his hands open. John nodded.

"You knew exactly how I'd react," Trip said. "You wanted Amanda free, but to do that you had to let Liz out. You had to make Liz think Amanda didn't have anyone else in the world she could trust." John nodded. Jessica looked at John like she could slap him.

"You used Amanda to help you with your own investigation?" she asked, furious. John looked down, ashamed.

"I had to get her out of the FBI building, Jess," John said quietly.

"You had to choose the lesser of two evils," Jeremiah said quietly, looking at John. Everyone turned and looked at the Vice-President. "You made the best choice you could given the circumstances." No one said anything for a second. John gave Jeremiah a small smile and a slight nod. The anger started to leave Jessica's face. Trip watched the two men, knowing they were talking about more than just Amanda.

"Of course, you have Liz under surveillance," Trip said. John grinned, and the entire table groaned.

Chapter 81

"Chet, be cool," John said. He pulled out his phone and hit the screen a few times. Chet watched, interested. A map popped up, with two dots on it. John looked at Chet proudly.

"I have nothing else to live for," Chet said with a smile on his face. He said it as a joke, but something inside of him felt strange. He shook it off and tried to see what John had on the phone.

"Hank bumped into Liz when we let her go and dropped a tracking device into her purse," John said, very proud of himself.

"What's the range on the device?" Chet asked. John stared at Chet blankly. "Maybe I do have something to live for." Chet didn't feel any better. Everyone continued to look at the phone and didn't notice him.

"That's strange," John said.

"What's wrong?" Jessica asked.

"She hasn't gone anywhere for a while," John replied. Trip and Jessica traded glances.

"The tracker was put in her purse?" Trip asked.

"Uh-huh," John replied, looking at the phone. He smacked the side of it. Jessica reached over and took it away.

"Why did you put it in the purse?" Jessica asked. John looked sullen like a school boy who had his comic book taken away.

"Because I told Hank to put it in there," John responded. Jessica looked at him. He sighed and continued. "She has to carry her gun somewhere," John said looking at her like it was the obvious answer.

"If it was a small gun, then she could wear it on her hip or in a smaller bag," Jessica answered. By the look on John's face, it was obvious he never considered that. "You thought she'd take that same purse everywhere?" John nodded. Trip closed his eyes. He looked like he might have an aneurysm.

"Hank's following Liz," John added. Everyone sighed in relief.

"Okay," Trip said, relieved. "What's the next step?"

"Put together enough to arrest Liz," John answered. "That's the next step. Somewhere down the road, I have to repair the problem with Amanda, but I don't know how." Jessica gave John a soft smile and put her hand on top of his.

"You'll figure it out," Jessica said. She looked down at his phone as it rang. She smiled and handed it to him. John looked at the caller ID and took the call.

"Something wrong?" John asked.

"I think I've lost Liz," Hank replied.

"I'll go find Amanda," John replied. "You try and find Liz."

"Gotcha," Hank said, and John disconnected. John looked at the table.

"Plan not working right?" Trip asked. "I'll get a team on Amanda." John shook his head.

"No," John said. "I'll go after her. You get a warrant for Liz and arrest her. I need to take care of Amanda." Trip nodded.

"Chet, Ron," Trip said.

"I'll drive," Ron said. "You get on the phone with whoever you're going to call." Chet nodded, and the two took off. John got up, and Jeremiah held up his hand for him to wait. They stepped away from the group. Jeremiah held his hand out to John. John shook it.

"I can never thank you, ma'boy," Jeremiah said. John shook his head.

"It was nothing," John replied. "Seriously, there was nothing I left out that would have helped us. There's no sense hurting people just because." Jeremiah nodded. John started out of the room.

"Hey!" Jessica yelled. John stopped, smiled, and turned. Jessica walked up to him. "Be careful."

"You act like she's going to shoot me or something," John said.

"There are days I want to shoot you."

"You know what I mean," John replied.

"Just be careful," she said, hugging him.

"Jessica, the last thing you have to worry about is Amanda aiming a gun at me," John said, having no idea how wrong he was.

Chapter 82

John headed out to his car and followed the directions to Amanda's blinking dot on the phone. She was on the move, and John had to keep changing course to follow her. He punched a button and heard the phone ringing through the car's speakers.

"John," Hank said.

"Is she moving?" John asked.

"I haven't seen her move all night," Hank responded.

"I'm less than five minutes from wherever she is going," John said. "That is if she doesn't keep moving."

"What do you want me to do?" Hank asked.

"Stay with her for now," John said and disconnected.

He followed the instructions on his phone for a few more minutes and then pulled the car into what seemed to be another abandoned warehouse.

"Seriously, how many of these things are there?" John mumbled to himself.

He saw Amanda approach a door on the side and open it. He walked over to the door, opened it carefully, and entered the warehouse and the darkness inside. He saw her go into a lighted hallway and followed her to it. When he got there, he saw her turn down another hallway. He continued to follow her. When he got to the intersection, he looked the way she went and saw only a door. John took a deep breath and headed toward the door.

When he reached the door, he peered into the window. There was a table in the middle of the floor, but there were sheets of plastic covering everything.

"It looks like that kill room off that TV show," he muttered to himself.

"Oh, it looks nothing like that show," the voice behind him said. John shook his head, still looking in the room.

"No, I think it does," he replied. It was then he realized no one should be behind him and he felt a gun in his ribs. "Oh, now do I feel stupid."

"No fast movements," the voice behind him said. It was female. John was pretty sure it was Liz. He no longer felt the gun in his ribs. "Raise your hands up as far as you can." John did. "Turn around very slowly, keeping your hands up, or I'll kill you." John did exactly what she said. Liz could see his gun. "One hand, two fingers, slowly draw it out, and drop it on the floor, or I kill you." John nodded and did exactly as she said. "Kick it over here." He did. She reached down and picked it up. "Now, knock on the door." He did. Amanda came over and opened the door. She looked at him with disgust.

"You!" she hissed.

"I guess this is a bad time to talk about your mom?" John asked.

"You know her mother?" Liz asked.

"I was married to her mother until she died," John responded. Liz smiled. She knew she had her new partner.

Chapter 83

"Open the door for him," Liz said. Amanda opened the door, and John stepped through, hands up. Liz handed Amanda John's gun. Amanda put the gun on a table. The table was over twelve feet away from John with Liz and Amanda standing between the gun and John.

"What's he doing here?" Amanda asked. "And, why do you have a gun pointed at him?"

"He snuck in here," Liz answered. "I don't know him. First, he's a FBI agent, and then, he's a lawyer? I think he's up to something."

"I'm trailing a killer," John said. Amanda glanced at Liz.

"Did he tell you that he talked to me at the FBI offices before he represented you as a lawyer?" Liz asked. Shock covered Amanda's face, and it slowly grew to anger. "Did he tell you that I told him I was dropping the charges?"

"Amanda, don't listen to her," John said.

"He can't lie," Amanda said softly. She looked at Liz. "He can't lie, so if you're telling me a story, it won't work."

"The only person telling a story is him," Liz answered, the gun trained on John. "Another man telling me whatever he thinks I want to hear to get his way."

"I'm going to ask him, and if he tells me you're lying, you'll put the gun down?" Amanda asked, trying to defuse the situation.

"He can't lie?" Liz asked.

"If he does, he starts itching and breaks out into hives," Amanda answered. Liz smiled.

"Ask him," Liz said, confidently. John began playing scenarios through his head. He could tell a lie, and he might not start itching, but just the thought of it caused him to almost scratch his arm. Besides, he didn't want his most pivotal moment with Amanda to be a lie.

"Liz is telling the truth," John said before Amanda could ask him. Amanda turned to John, shock covering her face. Liz was slightly astonished, but a cold smile covered her face. "I didn't tell you because I wanted the record to indicate that you fired me because you were mad at me. If anyone would have read it, perhaps it would have given you more protection."

"So, you were scheming?" Liz asked. John was frustrated.

"Of course I was scheming. It's what I do," John said. "I was trying to protect her, and she knows it."

"Who made you her protector!" Liz spat.

"Her mother," John said quietly. "Her mother wanted me to look after her."

"What about what she wants?" Liz asked, pointing to Amanda. Amanda was fuming. John could see it.

"Because I didn't know what she wanted," John said. "I could only go on what she told me. I was only trying to protect her." Liz shook her head.

"You're just like all the rest of them," Liz said with disdain. "You think you know what's best for her. You think we're incapable of taking care of ourselves. You don't trust us."

"Lady, quit spreading your crazy onto me," John said.

"Typical," she replied. "Once you hear something you don't like, you start degrading." She turned to Amanda. "Do you care for him?"

"I barely even know him," Amanda admitted. "For years, I thought he was trying to destroy my family, but for a few days, I thought I could trust him."

"And, now?" Liz asked. Amanda stared at John. She shook her head.

"And, now, I'm beginning to wonder if I wasn't right with my first impression of him," Amanda admitted.

"And, what was that?" Liz asked.

"That he needed to die for trying to destroy my family," Amanda said softly. John dropped his head.

"I'm so sorry, Sam," he said where they couldn't hear him. He looked back up and saw two women who wanted to kill him. This time, John didn't know what he was going to do.

Bruce Cosby
Secret Medical Facility

Chapter 84

Bruce had been patient the past few days. Arnold, Duck's lawyer that was currently representing Bruce, had told Bruce that his breakout would be coming soon. Bruce didn't know how, but he was getting ready. He was in peak physical condition. There was no pain from the wounds he had sustained from the gunshots he had received at the hands of both John and Chet.

He still remembered how it felt, to wake up in the bed some time ago and not be able to feel his legs from the pain medicine he was given. That's what he wanted now. He wanted his enemies to not be able to feel their legs. He wanted them to be powerless. He wanted them to be helpless as he carried out their death sentence. Bruce had a list in his mind of who was going first, and in what order. It was the only thing that kept him sane, in a manner of speaking.

He had studied. Oh, how he had studied. He knew exactly how to paralyze someone from the waist down. He knew exactly what he would do as he towered over them, punishing them, and then, at a time of his choosing, ending their life.

Bruce knew all the guards and the attendants, but there were two here today that he didn't recognize. Bruce really thought they might be Italian. Bruce began to feel giddy. He began to feel the rage course through his body. He began to feel the euphoric high. He knew it would be soon. Suddenly, his door sprang open, and Bruce was feeling the mania spread through him like fire running through his veins.

"It's time," one of the attendants that Bruce didn't recognize said. Bruce stuck his wrists out.

"Be gentle, fellas," Bruce said, feeling the madness sweep through him. "I bruise easily." He felt the need to giggle but fought it off. The two attendants paused but quickly locked him up and led him down the same hallway that he was taken when he met his father some time back. Soon he was led out the back door and into a van. Within minutes he saw he was clear of the facility. He was free. An evil grin covered his face.

"Hold still, sir," one of the attendants said, unlocking his restraints. Within seconds, Bruce was free. "There's a change of clothes in the back and the boots you asked for." Bruce nodded and scurried to the back of the van to get out of the hospital clothes.

"Just my size," he said happily as he dressed. He admired the boots on his feet. They were heavy military boots with a steel toe in the front.

"Where to, sir?" one of the attendants asked. Bruce smiled, a smile that one can only imagine if you saw a snake smile, and gave them an address. Within the hour, the van arrived at the address. "Do you require any assistance?"

"No," Bruce replied, thinking of all the ways he was going to make his victim suffer. "You boys have performed admirably." Bruce exited the van in an alley less than a block from his target. The van pulled away, and Bruce watched it go. He checked his coat and found the lock picking tools that he needed. It wouldn't be long now. It wouldn't be long until Bruce killed one that was close to John and then . . . and only then, John would climb back in the bottle, and hopefully drown. Bruce couldn't help himself. He giggled, and headed down the street.

Liz's Kill Room
New York, New York

Chapter 85

Liz trained her gun at John. John tried to think of anything to get out of this mess, but nothing came to mind. He looked over at Amanda and could see the pleasure on her face. John had badly miscalculated. He had known that Amanda hadn't truly trusted him, but he thought she would give him the benefit of the doubt. The look on Amanda's face was one of cold satisfaction. She told him a few days ago she would see him dead. Actually, that wasn't true. She had said she would kill him. A thought formed in John's mind.

"Amanda," John began.

"Oh, isn't this sweet," Liz said, shaking her head sadly. "You're trying to plead for your life. Don't you get it? We're tired of being taken advantage of." Amanda looked at Liz.

"It was your father, wasn't it?" Amanda asked, and Liz nodded.

"He was always trying to control me. He ran my life. He never gave me what I wanted," Liz replied.

"He told you no, you nut!" John yelled. Liz gave John a withering look and turned to Amanda.

"Would you like the honor of killing yours?" Liz asked. Amanda nodded. John, for a split second, got a flicker of hope inside of him. The look on Amanda's face was pure hatred. John, desperate, looked around for anything. Amanda had the look of someone that was ready to kill. Liz handed John's gun to Amanda who took it and aimed it at John.

"I want you to think of every evil thing your father ever did to you," Liz egged Amanda on. Fury washed over Amanda. "I want you to think of the biggest sin he committed and how he tried to get out of it."

John decided if he was going to die, he was going out trying and not standing around doing nothing.

"That's right Amanda," John said. "You think of everything your father did." Amanda's dead, blank eyes stared back at John. John swallowed and continued. "You remember what he did to your mother. How he used her, and left her. Think how he raised you. How did he raise you, Amanda? Like a daughter or something to remind him of her? Remember every single second of it, and then, you do what you have to do. You just remember one thing. Your mother, who never knew you, who never met you, wrote a journal for you. She loved you more than your father did, and she never spent a second with you. If you think shooting me will let all that hatred and anger go, then you shoot me. You kill me, and I won't try to stop you. But, if you don't, if you'll give me a chance, I'll help you do what you want. We'll get him, Amanda, for her." Liz's head whipped around toward John.

"You must be insane," Liz said, not sure what was going on. She turned to Amanda. "You've got to kill him. It's the only way you'll ever release all of that inside of you. You've got to do it!"

"No," Amanda said, shaking her head, her gun still trained on John.

"He killed your mother, he's got to die," Liz said and began to raise her gun toward John. John shut his eyes, hoping this didn't hurt as bad as the last time he got shot. A shot rang out. John didn't feel anything. He opened one eye and saw Amanda standing over Liz's body. Liz appeared to be dead.

"You got it wrong," Amanda said. "I wanted the man responsible for killing my mother to die." Amanda looked over at John who was trying to find a cool way to make sure he hadn't wet his pants. "What happened to her isn't his fault. And, I know whose fault it is." John took the gun from Amanda and grabbed Liz's gun, just in case.

Amanda didn't even notice, still staring at the body. John got his phone and called in the shooting. He went back to Amanda. She turned to him, and John saw a scared girl in front of him, not the twenty-something lady he had seen for weeks. Tears formed in her eyes, and she collapsed on his shoulder, crying. She continued to cry, and John continued to hold her as the ambulances and police cars arrived.

Chapter 86

Jessica arrived on the scene a few minutes later. She searched frantically for John. She finally saw him sitting on the back of an ambulance. That didn't surprise her. She had noticed in the years of working with John, he, or someone close to him, ended up sitting on the back of an ambulance at the end of cases. No, what threw her was Amanda sitting beside him, a blanket over them, and her head on John's shoulder. If that wasn't enough to shake Jessica, John looked absolutely comfortable with Amanda, almost like a father and daughter. John saw Jessica and started to rise. Jessica quickly shook her head, waved, and headed off to find Trip.

She only took a few steps before she saw him talking to Hank. Hank saw Jessica, gave her a nod, and headed off. Where Trip was standing, it was obvious that he had seen Jessica watching John and Amanda, that and the amused look on his face.

"I wouldn't believe it if I hadn't seen it with my own eyes," Trip said softly as Jessica approached him.

"What happened?" Jessica asked.

"Liz tried to get Amanda to kill her father for all the terrible things he had done to her," Trip answered. Jessica looked at him sharply. Trip grinned. "Liz assumed John was Amanda's father. In the end, he might just be." Jessica turned back and looked at the two of them. Trip looked down at the ground, shifted uncomfortably, and looked at Jessica. "It's natural to be a little jealous," Trip said softly. Jessica turned around with amusement on her face. "Besides, maybe he really is the fatherly type, and you could have one of your own." Jessica's face fell a little. She gave Trip a sad smile.

"I don't think I can," Jessica answered. "Besides, do you really think the two of us need to raise a child?" Trip looked embarrassed, and was grasping for words. "It's okay, Trip," she said, smiling at him.

"Well," Trip began. Jessica shook her head, stopping him before he said something worse.

"Don't you dare say I could be like a mother to her," Jessica said. "I'm what, twelve, eleven years older than her? I could be her big sister." Jessica turned back, looking at the two again. "Although, Sam would have wanted me to be her godmother." Jessica turned back to face Trip. Confusion covered Trip's face. "She would have been twelve or so when we first met, so it could have worked," Jessica said defensively. Trip smiled and looked back down at the ground. He looked back up at Jessica, seriousness on his face.

"What happens to him if they can't make whatever they have work?" Trip asked, scared of the answer. Jessica set her jaw; tears were fighting to roll down her cheeks.

"They don't get that option," Jessica responded flatly. "We both know what Sam would have wanted, and that's what has to happen."

"Jessica," Trip began softly. He stopped as he saw a single tear fall from her eye.

"They don't have a choice, Trip," she said softly but fiercely. "We owe her that." With that, tears fell. Trip did something he never did. He opened his arms to his agent, no, his friend. He held Jessica as she cried.

"We do owe her that," Trip said, not knowing if he was agreeing with her to make her feel better, or trying to convince himself. Trip watched Amanda and John still sitting, not saying a word, and wondered how anyone who didn't know John could form the relationship that Jessica thought Sam would have wanted them to have.

Chapter 87

Ron and Chet came up to John and Amanda sitting on the ambulance.

"Thank you," Ron said to both Amanda and John.

"It was Dwayne that killed your mom, right?" John asked, confused as to why Ron was thanking them.

"Yeah, but because of Liz, I spent a lot of time spinning my wheels on this case," Ron replied, looking over at the coroner's vehicle. He turned back to the group. "Besides, the people she killed deserve closure as well." John nodded. "I'm going to do the paperwork on this one." Ron started to walk off.

"I'll do it," John said, stopping Ron in his tracks. Ron turned around and looked at Amanda and then at John.

"Well, this is obviously very official," Amanda said, getting up. John looked worried. "Don't you start mothering me," she said directly to John. Chet smiled.

"You're just like her," Chet said softly. John had to nod in agreement. Amanda shook her head.

"I'm leaving before you two start crying," Amanda said, smiling. She turned toward John. "I'll talk to you soon." John nodded, and Amanda walked off.

"You okay, Boss?" Chet asked, worried. John nodded.

"I'm better than I've been in a long time," he answered and meant it. Things finally felt right to John. "It's good to have the whole team together."

"It's good to have you back, John," Chet said. Chet couldn't shake the feeling that something wasn't right. John was oblivious, watching Amanda leave and then wondering what Trip and Jessica were talking about. John shrugged, turned toward his friend, and noticed the worried look on Chet's face.

"What's got you looking like that?" John asked.

"I don't know," Chet replied, shaking his head. John began to study Chet. Chet sighed. "Okay, okay, if you must know, I had a bad feeling about this case." John clapped his friend on the shoulder.

"But the case is over, and you feel okay now," John replied. Chet looked at John and slightly shook his head.

"That's just it," he replied. "The feeling hasn't gone away."

"Maybe it's gas," John said, smiling.

"Maybe," Chet replied. He didn't think it was. In fact, he was worried. He was afraid this was their last case together, and he didn't know why.

"See you later?" John asked, pulling Chet out of his thoughts. Chet thought for a second. "You know what? Take tomorrow off, and get out of this funk. Ron and I have got this," John added. Chet nodded and watched John walk back toward Jessica and Trip. Chet felt a chill, looked around, shook his head, and headed to his car. When he got there, he took a look at the three talking and wondered why he thought he wouldn't see them again.

Chapter 88

Kenneth sat, wringing his hands. He had lost so much over the past few months. His two friends sat quietly, watching him. From time to time, they would take a sip of the hot beverage in front of them, but neither said anything. Neither of them had a clue what to say. Neither man could ever say Kenneth wasn't dedicated to the cause. No one had given as much as he had, and he was prepared to lose more. Kenneth looked over at Archibald.

"You've lost a daughter over all of this," Kenneth said quietly.

"You've lost the presidency, your father, and your wife," Archibald answered just as quietly. "You don't have to do this. We aren't asking you to."

"There are other ways," Duck added. "We've obviously misjudged Fowler again. He's the one we should take out."

"That's not the answer," Archibald said, "We can't have a FBI agent killed. That will do nothing but bring down more heat on us." Archibald shook his head. Kenneth always mapped out each of his kills. They had been numerous, but they had always left no way to come back to the group. Archibald sometimes thought Duck had fantasies of being a mafia leader similar to ones in the movies, just killing anyone, whenever, not caring what the consequences were. There were times Archibald wondered if he and Kenneth shouldn't end their relationship with Duck.

"Bruce will probably take care of him for us anyway," Duck said. Both Kenneth and Archibald made the same disgusted sound.

"There's one who went off the reservation," Kenneth said. "I think we should agree to never use him again, upon penalty of death." Archibald nodded in agreement. Duck felt his stomach lurch. He was truly alone now. The mafia had told him not to have an FBI agent killed, and now, his own group of power had told him not to use Bruce. Duck hadn't felt this way since before he climbed to the top of the mob. Duck sat quietly thinking about his options. He had to stop the murder, but could he? As Duck thought, Bruce and Archibald continued their discussions, ignoring Duck.

"We've always said the group comes first," Kenneth went on. Archibald slowly nodded. "We need to end this. We need to cut out this cancer." Archibald sat up straight.

"Let's think about this," Archibald began. Kenneth waved his hand.

"I've already decided, Archibald," Kenneth answered. "Will you help me?"

"You know I will," Archibald answered softly and proudly. He wished Kenneth had been his son. They turned to Duck who was off in his own thoughts.

"Duck, I need you to put a hit out on my daughter," Kenneth said quietly. Duck barely heard Kenneth, and when he did, he played it back in his head to make sure he had heard what he thought he had.

"Kenneth, if I put this out, there is very little chance I could cancel it," Duck said. "I want you to think on it for a few days. Give it at least 48 hours, and if that's what you want, then I'll put the hit out." Archibald nodded.

"That's a good idea," he said to Kenneth. "Trying to cancel a hit is nearly impossible." Duck's stomach churned.

"I have some business if we are done," Duck said quickly. "I'll await your call," he said to Kenneth, and with that, he left. Archibald shook his head as he watched him leave.

"There's days..." he began and then trailed off.

"Are you thinking we should end our partnership with him?" Kenneth asked. Archibald turned with a smile on his face.

"It's something I've wondered, but we don't need a mob war," Archibald answered. Kenneth nodded. The two men sat in silence, lost in their thoughts.

Outside, Duck desperately called Bruce. After the third try, Bruce answered.

"Bruce, cancel the hit! Don't do it!!" Duck screamed into the phone. Duck swore he heard laughing on the other end.

"Too late," was the only reply he heard before the line went dead. Duck redialed, but the phone call went straight to voicemail. Duck got into his car. He had to think. There was only one place he might be safe now, but if he did what he was contemplating, then his life was over as he knew it, but at least he'd be alive.

Chet's Brownstone
New York, New York

Chapter 89

Chet left his brownstone to run some errands. After his car pulled away, a man walked up to the locked door and worked on the lock for a few minutes. The door to Chet's brownstone opened, and a figure stepped inside from the darkness. He looked around the dwelling and closed the door gently behind him. There were no physical signs of the break in on the door. He spied the item he was looking for and slowly walked across the floor until he found the katana that was displayed. He stopped in front of it and stared at his reflection in the sword. Bruce could see his teeth from his smile on the sword blade. He left the blade and went to work in the home. He disabled the land line phone and turned off the electricity at the main breaker. He looked around to make sure he had not disturbed anything and returned to the living room. There, he picked up the sword, took his position behind the door, and waited.

Bruce listened for a few minutes and heard absolutely nothing. He crept over to the door and cautiously opened it. He heard the noise of the city and quietly closed the door. He didn't move; he just stood and listened. Quiet. Total, complete quiet. Bruce smiled his sick demented smile. His blues eyes danced at the thought of what was about to happen and how much fun he was going to have at whatever decibel he wanted to. It's good to be me, Bruce thought.

Ron McGuire, That Afternoon
New York FBI Offices

Chapter 90

Ron was looking over his case file one last time.
He had promised his mom that he would catch her killer,
and he had. Well, he and the team had. Ron couldn't help
but feel a little regret that he hadn't been the one to kill his
mother's killer, but justice had been served in his mind.
Now, there was just one more loose end to tie up in his life,
but he had told himself long ago that it would take a
miracle to figure out who was to blame for his stepfather's
death.

Ron's cell phone vibrated, and he looked down at a
text. The text told him to call the phone number that had
just texted him when he was alone if he wanted to know the
truth about his stepfather. Emotions ran through Ron,
emotions he thought he had repressed long ago. Ron
picked up the file he had been looking at and took it to
John's office.

"You wanted to see this before it got turned in?"
Ron asked John, holding up the case file. John nodded. "If
you don't have anything else, I'm going to take off." John
shook his head.

"I'm good. Is Chet gone?" John asked.

"He took off a little bit ago, he had a campaign
tonight," Ron answered with a smile on his face. John
shook his head, smiling.

"I assume that is something to do with computers?"
John asked.

"Yes, John, computers are involved," Ron
answered. "And the internet and other gamers." John
waved for him to stop. "See you tomorrow, Boss," Ron
said and started to walk away.

"Ron," John said, stopping Ron in his tracks. Ron
stuck his head back in the office. "You did good work on

this. I'm glad you came to New York." Ron smiled, nodded, and headed out of the office. He had just thought it would take a miracle to find out who had killed his stepfather, and now it seemed like a miracle was being provided.

Chapter 91

Ron walked out of the foxhole, and made sure the door was closed and the hall empty. He recognized the number from his stepfather's phone. It was one of the phone numbers he had never been able to run down. Ron had only known tragedy when it came to parents. His father had died on the job in Detroit. His mother had been a victim of Dwayne Sapp, and his stepfather had had his neck broken a few years ago. His father's killer had been killed on the spot by his father's partner, Dwayne had been killed by Liz, but his stepdad's killer was still out there.

Ron's stepfather, Bill, had never tried to take his father's place. Bill never pressured Ron but asked if Ron would take Bill's last name. After Ron's mom decided to take Bill's last name, Ron thought it was only right he did as well. Bill had been there for Ron when his mom had died, and that's what mattered to Ron. Bill had taught Ron that blood didn't necessarily make someone family. Ron knew that Bill had some vices: gambling and drinking, mostly. Ron had promised himself he was going to find his mother's and stepfather's killers, and now, he might actually have the chance to accomplish his goal.

"Hello," he spoke. He was fighting to keep himself calm.

"Ron McGuire?" the voice on the other end asked hesitantly.

"Who is this?" Ron asked, trying to keep control of himself.

"Ron, you don't know me, but I can help you," the voice on the other end said. "I can give you what you want. I can tell you who killed William McGuire, or the man you used to call Dad." Ron felt the air escape from his body. "I'll tell you everything, but you have to trust me. Time is critical."

"Who is this?" Ron asked again.

"My name is Robert Mariotti Jr, but you probably know me as Duck," Duck replied.

"Exactly why should I trust a word you say?" Ron asked.

"I'll tell you everything that happened to your father, and then, you can make up your own mind," Duck offered. "But, if you believe me, then you have to do something for me."

"Why would I ever do anything for you?" Ron asked.

"Because if you don't listen to me, I'm going to let one of your friends die," Duck replied. "Bruce Cosby is on the loose, and he has his eyes set on one of your friends. You listen to what I say, and I'll tell you who and where. You don't and I let Bruce kill one of your teammates. Do we understand each other?"

"What's stopping me from hanging up with you and telling the team?" Ron asked, looking back at the door of the foxhole.

"You want revenge, and you haven't got it yet. Have you, Ronald?" Duck said. Ron stopped in midstride. He had decided to go back in and tell John what was going on, but that comment changed his mind.

"I'm listening," Ron said.

Chapter 92

"First off, I have to apologize to you," Duck began. "It's my fault that your father is dead."

"What do you mean?" Ron snapped.

"Your stepfather liked to gamble," Duck began. He paused, wondering how Ron was going to react to what he was about to tell him.

"Go on," Ron said through gritted teeth.

"Your stepfather owed me quite a bit of money. I had met Bruce sometime back but had never used his services before. Apparently, he had some pent up frustration that day because he wanted to let go of some hostility. He had just got passed up for a special team his father had put together, and now he had to do something." Duck paused, carefully selecting his words. "Bruce came to me, asking if there was someone that needed persuading. Your father was in rather deep and I thought it was time someone paid him a visit to remind him that he still owed me."

"What happened?" Ron asked, knowing his stepfather's ultimate fate but not the steps that led there.

"You have to understand. All I wanted was an understanding. He owed me. That was all." Duck was speaking fast and licking his lips, trying to get the whole story out before Ron hung up and Duck found himself in a worse situation. "Bruce was supposed to go explain things to him, and if he didn't listen, Bruce was supposed to rough him up a bit." Ron was very silent. "Are you there?"

"Go on," Ron said softly.

"Well, apparently your father had decided enough was enough. He told Bruce that he was done. Your father said he would pay back whatever he owed, and Bruce could just give him the beating. You have to understand, Bruce was just nuts and your father knew it. Your father knew Bruce just wanted to beat someone, and that's what he did. Bruce took out all of his frustrations on your father. He beat him unmercifully. When it was over, Bruce realized what he did and was afraid he would be found out. Your father was unconscious, and Bruce called me. He told me what he had done." Duck paused.

"Finish it," Ron said, his voice barely a whisper.

"I tried, Ron. You have to believe me," Duck said, almost pleading. "I had Bruce check himself over. He had worn gloves. There was no trace evidence on him that couldn't be destroyed. There was no skin under your father's nails. But, Bruce insisted that your father had seen him and had to be taken care of." Duck paused. "I've been around this element all my life, but Bruce…" Duck trailed off.

"He broke my father's neck and enjoyed it," Ron said, not asked.

"Exactly," Duck said. "Bruce told me he would take your stepfather's debt in return for my silence of what had happened. At first, it seemed too good to be true. My friends and I figured out everything that was coming from the information Bruce supplied. Well, that and we planned it all, and I soon rose to the top of the game."

"So, what do you want from me?" Ron asked, barely keeping the emotion from his voice.

"I need you to get rid of Bruce," Duck said.

"And if I do?" Ron asked.

"I'll owe you a favor," Duck said softly.

"Where is he?" Ron asked immediately.

"He's headed to your friend's house. The one called Chet," Duck replied. Ron clicked off the call and ran to the garage. He never once stopped to consider telling John and Jessica.

John Fowler
New York FBI Offices

Chapter 93

John sat at his desk, looking over the case file one last time. He wanted to make sure everything was correct. This may have been the only time he had ever worried about that in his entire life. Most case files he pawned off on others. The only one he had ever cared about before was Sam's, and in the end, Jessica and Chet had completed it. Now, he had a file in his hands that led back to Amanda. John wasn't sure how he was supposed to feel about Amanda. She wasn't his daughter, but she was Sam's, and at the end of the day, he thought that made her his responsibility.

"Thinking about her, aren't you?" Jessica's voice cut through John's thoughts. He looked up and saw Jessica leaning on the doorframe of his office. John nodded. "You know some newlyweds would take offense to their husbands thinking about another woman."

"Do you think that these husbands are usually thinking about their deceased wife's child she never knew?" John asked. Jessica smiled at John.

"I doubt any of those husbands think of any the things you do," Jessica answered. John grinned and closed the case file. "You ready to go home?" she asked. John nodded, got up, and headed toward his wife. He wondered if kissing her here would violate some laws that human resources had on file. He decided it was worth the risk. He leaned in to kiss her when he noticed Trip leading Amanda through the door to their offices. John paused mid-lean, causing Jessica to give him a look like he had lost his mind. She turned and followed his gaze. She saw Amanda, and Jessica felt her heart leap inside. Amanda didn't look happy, but she did seem to be there of her own will.

"This young lady would like to talk to you," Trip said. He leaned against the desk that was in the center of the room where John usually worked. John and Jessica came out of the office but didn't get too close to Amanda, giving her space.

"This room's a little weird. Don't you think?" Amanda asked, looking around. She pointed toward Chet's computer setup. "I mean, there's all sorts of technology here, but over there," pointing towards John's and Jessica's office, "it looks like something out of the 90s." John looked around with a slight smile on his face and nodded.

"We are who we are," John said. Amanda rolled her eyes. John couldn't help himself. He laughed and began to tear up at the same time. She looked so much like her mother in that instance. Amanda turned to Trip.

"See, this is the problem," she said to Trip. "He's going to tear up every time I do something that reminds him of her." Trip gave a knowing smile and shrugged.

"He loved her," Trip answered simply. Amanda turned back and looked at Jessica for help. Jessica shrugged. Amanda sighed.

"I know," she said. "That's why I'm here.

Chapter 94

"I can help you get him," Amanda said very quietly. John remained leaning against the glass wall of his office with his arms crossed. After she spoke, he straightened, uncrossed his arms, and walked over toward her. Jessica was very near tears. She knew what a big step this was for these two. John walked up very close to her but made sure to respect her space.

"Do you understand what you're saying and what he would do to you if he knew?" John asked, starting to reach out to put his hand on her shoulder but stopping himself. Amanda noticed and smiled.

"I know exactly how vindictive he can be," she answered.

"I can't guarantee your safety," John said quietly. Trip looked like he had been hit with a ton of bricks, and Jessica nearly gasped. John hurried on. "I couldn't protect Sam, and I won't lie to you. I don't know if anyone can stop him when he sets his mind to it." Amanda looked over at Trip who looked ready to strangle John, but at the same time, he begrudgingly agreed with what John said. She looked back to John.

"You just can't lie. Can you?" she asked softly. John shook his head, tears in his eyes. "Do you think she loved me?" Tears streamed down both of their faces. John didn't trust himself to speak, but he managed to nod. "Do you think she thought I was alive?" John pulled in his bottom lip and chewed on it. He looked at Amanda and took a deep breath.

"All I know for sure is she never said anything to me that would indicate you were. I suspect now that she wondered, but she didn't dare say anything for fear of what might happen to me. She knew what I would have done if she had told me that you were alive. I think in her mind, she hoped. She had no proof, but she wondered. Now, I can see that. I think if she ever had a shred of proof we would have tried to find you, but there was nothing, Amanda. There was nothing."

"I think he broke me," Amanda said quietly. John smiled and glanced at Jessica.

"Someone really smart once told me that I wasn't broken, just bent," John replied, wanting to take Amanda's hand but thought she wouldn't appreciate that. Amanda looked at him. John didn't know where the instinct came from, but he thought he should hug her. He didn't but did continue. "Sometimes, when we're in bad spots, we think we're broken, but I think she's right. We're just bent." Amanda stood there, nodding. She looked at John, John looked back, not sure what to do.

"This is where you're supposed to hug me, John," she said quietly. Jessica burst out into laughter. Everyone turned to look at her.

"Oh, come on!" she said, tears flowing down her face but happiness covering it as well. "We all know she sounded exactly like Sam." Amanda turned toward John for confirmation. John grinned and nodded. He opened his arms, and Amanda hugged him. John began to cry freely. Trip walked out of the room, complaining about allergies affecting his eyes. Jessica came over to the two, standing just outside of them. Amanda took one arm off John and held it out. Jessica hugged both of them.

"I want to help catch my mom's killer," Amanda said to them. "I know that Bruce killed her, and it was supposedly Archibald's idea, but I know what my dad did to her led to her eventually dying."

"You've got it, sweetie," Jessica answered. John looked at Jessica. "I can call my goddaughter sweetie if I want to."

"Goddaughter?" John asked. Jessica looked at Amanda who shrugged and then back to John. "If Sam had a daughter, don't you think she'd make me the godmother?" John smiled at the two of them. He was happy about all that had happened, but he still felt like an outsider. Amanda turned her head and looked at John, the same way Sam used to when it seemed to John she could read him like a book. John swore Sam had the same abilities he did, but Sam denied it. She said she could tell what he was thinking, but he was the only person. Amanda smiled at John.

"I guess that would have made you my stepdad then. Wouldn't it?" she asked. Jessica took her hands, clasped them together where the middle finger lay on her nose and her index fingers laid on her lips. Tears streamed down Jessica's face. John didn't say a word. The tears in his eyes and the set of his jaw said it all. Amanda hugged him tightly as John looked at Jessica who was smiling through her tears. "I'm sorry for all the trouble I've been, John…" Amanda said softly. She pulled away and looked at him. "I'm a little old to start calling you Dad." John nodded. A huge smile broke across Amanda's face, the same kind that used to cover Sam's when she pulled something over on him. "Dad." Jessica began to laugh and hugged the both of them.

Trip watched from outside through the open door, thinking how perfectly this had all ended. The three of them deserved happiness. Somewhere in the back of his mind came a thought that this was about the time in movies or a TV show that something would go terribly wrong and change their lives forever. Trip shook his head, pushing the thought from his mind. It was then his cell phone lit up, and his and the entire team's lives went up in flames.

Chapter 95

"Assistant Director Trip," he said, not recognizing the phone number.

"Sir," the nervous voice said on the other end. "This is to inform you and your agents that Bruce Cosby has escaped our facility." Trip turned to look at the three in the other room as the blood drained from his face. The voice on the other line told Trip what they thought had happened, but Trip wasn't listening. The phone began to fall out of his hand. John looked over toward Trip at that exact second, and it didn't take John's abilities for him to know something was wrong. Trip's eyes met John's.

"Bruce," Trip mumbled softly, and John knew just as the same as if Trip had told him.

The world suddenly stopped for John. John could hear his heartbeat in his ears. He couldn't hear anything else. It was then he noticed that everything seemed to be going black, and he wondered why Trip, with his hand outstretched seemed to be turning sideways and running toward John. He felt hands grab at him, but they couldn't stop him from crashing to the floor.

"What's wrong with him?" Amanda asked, terrified.

"PTSD," Jessica answered, slapping John's face in an attempt to get him to open his eyes. She pointed toward her office, never taking her eyes off John. "Get my purse off my desk and bring it to me." Amanda did as she was told. Jessica quickly reached into her purse, pulled out a vial of something, and opened it. Amanda's eyes quickly began to water, and Trip gagged. John made a face, and shook his head, opening his eyes.

"What died?" he asked weakly.

"I thought you had for a minute," Amanda said, finally realizing that she was holding his hand. Confused, John looked at her.

"Do you remember anything?" Jessica asked. John turned white, and Jessica started to reach for the vial again. John shook his head.

"I'm good," John said quickly. "Sorry about that."

"What made him do that?" Amanda asked, still confused.

"I think Trip found out something about Bruce," Jessica said, eyeing John as she spoke. Trip nodded.

"He escaped," John said softly. "He's out. Isn't he?"

"You don't know?" Amanda asked, even more confused.

"Sweetie, Bruce nearly killed him," Jessica gently explained. "He jumps about twenty feet when a car backfires." John shot Jessica a look, and Trip shot John a look. John tried to appear sheepish and decided it was time to get up. He began to get up, and everyone tried to help at once.

"I got it," John said a little too forcefully. Trip and Jessica both smiled, knowing he was okay.

"Try to help a guy out, and you get your head chewed off," Amanda said with a look on her face that made John smile. "Let me guess. I look just like her." John nodded and shrugged. He suddenly jumped up.

"What?" Jessica asked.

"Chet and Ron," John said. "They don't know about Bruce!" The color drained from Jessica's face as they all ran for their phones.

Outside of Chet's Brownstone
New York, New York

Chapter 96

Chet parked his car in his normal spot outside of his brownstone. He got out of the car and looked up at the New York skyline. For some reason, he couldn't get it out of his head that he might never see this scene again. Chet shook his head and started toward the door when he remembered the bag of groceries he had left in the car. He went back to get the groceries. As he picked up the bag, he saw his neighbor Mrs. Williams trying to fight with her two young sons and get her own groceries out of the car.

"Can I give you a hand, Mrs. Williams?" Chet called. Mrs. Williams looked up, saw Chet, and smiled.

"Please," she said. Chet nodded, put his groceries back in his car, took his coat off and threw it inside the open door, and closed and locked the car door. As he walked over to help Mrs. Williams, the phone in the coat pocket vibrated as it received an incoming call. The name John came across the screen of Chet's phone. Oblivious of his own present danger, Chet helped Mrs. Williams with her sons and the groceries.

John Fowler
New York FBI Offices

Chapter 97

"I can't get Chet!" John screamed across the room. Panic was setting in, and John thought he was about to have another episode. John saw the room spin and would have crashed to the ground, but the thought of his friend being attacked by that maniac kept John upright. He did go down to one knee to balance himself, but he quickly pulled himself back up. John grabbed the desk phone, while Trip was on his cell phone screaming at someone to assemble everyone they had to find Bruce. Jessica came out of her office with a protective vest on and a shotgun. She had bad intentions.

"Hold it, Jessica," Trip said as calmly as he could. "You're not going anywhere. When I find all four of you, you're going under lock and key. NO arguments!" Trip went back to his phone call, and Jessica stood there, mad. John knew that Jessica would cool off at some point, and besides that, Trip was right. This was a time to make sure they were safe, not go off half-cocked. Besides, if anyone was going out there hunting Bruce, it was going to be him. He just hadn't had the guts to tell Jessica yet.

John had dialed Ron's cellphone during all the commotion and had just now noticed it had gone to voicemail. He slammed the phone down in frustration, nearly breaking the receiver. John felt someone beside him and saw it was Amanda.

"What can I do?" she asked.

"Just keep redialing the number on that phone," John said, pointing to the phone he had almost broke. Amanda nodded, and John began to call Chet again on his cellphone. John prayed he got ahold of his friend before it was too late.

Outside of Chet's Brownstone
New York, New York

Chapter 98

Chet waved to Mrs. Williams as he left her to fight with her two boys. He walked back to his car, unlocked the car door, grabbed his coat and his groceries, shut and locked the door, and started to his home. Chet felt the phone vibrating in his coat pocket as he was trying to get his keys. The phone seem to vibrate insistently as he fumbled for his keys in his pocket. Chet got the keys finally and began to unlock the door when the phone stopped vibrating. He got the keys out of the door and back in his pocket. He reached to open the door when the phone began to ring again.

"John must have broken his DVR and needs help," Chet said out loud to no one. He got his phone out of his coat pocket and flipped the light switch as he walked in the door. The lights didn't come on.

"Must have blown a breaker," he said. Chet used the light from his cell phone to help him navigate through the apartment to his kitchen where he placed the groceries on the table. He unclipped his gun from his belt and put it in the bowl where he kept it when he was home. He used the light to find the flashlight he kept in the cupboards. He got the flashlight out when the phone began to vibrate again.

"What?" he answered, exasperated with the constant phone calls, as he tried to get the flashlight on. A beam of light cut across the darkness.

"Chet, are you okay?" John nearly screamed through the phone.

"I'm fine, John," Chet answered. "Is there a city-wide power outage or something?"

"What are you talking about?" John asked.

"The lights are off. I assumed that's why you were calling so insistently," Chet replied, making his way back over to the front room. For a second, Chet thought he saw something in the darkness but shrugged it off. No one was in his house. The door had been locked when he got home, so no one could have broken in. None of the electronics were missing, and nothing was out of order. He turned around and noticed something was missing from its spot. Chet was puzzled. Of all things to steal, why that?

"What do you mean the lights are off?" John asked, his voice cutting through Chet's thoughts.

"None of the lights are on," Chet answered, his voice trailing off. He had his flashlight pointed where his sword used to be sitting. It was gone.

"Chet, listen to me! Bruce has broken out of prison!" John said frantically. It finally dawned on Chet what was going on in his home. He felt fear grip his thoat.

"John," Chet whispered frantically, afraid to move. "I think he's here." Chet started to move when for a split second, he felt the greatest pain in his back, and then, he felt nothing. He was surprised by the sensation. He was even more surprised when he realized his legs couldn't take the weight of his body as he fell. The phone and flashlight pitched forward out of his hand. Chet felt himself hit the ground somewhere around the waist up. He wondered why he suddenly couldn't feel his feet. It was then he felt pressure on his back. He heard John screaming on the phone. It was several feet away from Chet. Chet was speechless. The flashlight had rolled across the floor and now laid at such an angle that he could make out a reflection in his TV. In the reflection, he saw himself on the floor with a sword sticking out of his back. Chet realized that as bad as that was, that was the least of his problems. A figure began to squat behind him, admiring what looked to be his work. Chet saw Bruce's reflection in the TV and knew now why he had been having these premonitions for the past few hours. Today was the day Chet was going to die. Chet watched as Bruce gave his famous creepy smile.

"John," Bruce said in a mocking voice. Chet could see Bruce trace his finger over the butt of a gun that was tucked in the waistband of his pants. "Chet can't come to the phone right now. He was naughty, and we have to discuss his punishment." Bruce began to giggle, and then, his mad laughter began to ricochet through the dark room.

Across the city, John stared at the phone, horrified and helpless. There was nothing he could do to save his friend. Chet was going to die.

John Fowler
New York FBI Offices

Chapter 99

John felt his own legs give out. The room seemed to spin, and then, there was pain on the side of his head. He was trying to figure out why the room was sideways all of a sudden. One word flashed through his mind. Bruce! His mind tried to work, but it was frozen. He wasn't seeing right out of his eyes. He noticed people moving, but for the life of him, he couldn't figure out they were. He saw three people all rushing toward him.

John tried to get up, but his body just didn't cooperate. He focused and tried to make his mind work. That was when he noticed there was a fourth person in the room. She was just behind everyone. It was Sam.

"Get up!" she yelled at him.

"I can't," he said but knew he wasn't speaking. What was going on?

"John, you have to get up, or Chet is going to die!" she said frantically.

"Will you take care of him?" John asked. Sam shook her head.

"John, he doesn't have to die! You can still save him!" Sam looked desperate. All John could think was how Chet was in his apartment alone with Bruce. John remembered how Chet had loved his home because it was virtually soundproof. He could play his games or music as loud as he wanted, and no one complained. He wasn't interrupted by others and the sounds of New York. John was thinking how right now, that sounded like a crypt that Chet was about to be buried in.

"John, you have to get up! You have to stall him!" Sam was screaming at him.

"Why?" John asked, near tears but knowing he was neither talking nor crying. "I can't save him."

"You don't have to! Think about it! Where's Ron?"

And, with that, John's mind finally cut loose. It started to process everything he had known and observed about Ron. It started making all the connections that he already knew about. A map was forming in John's head, and it kept going back to two things. One, why had Ron left Special Forces so young? Two, what had happened to Ron's stepfather, the one who had had his neck broken? Neck broke? And, then, it all slammed together. John looked up and saw Sam give him the nod she used to give him when she saw the look of confidence on his face when he broke a case.

"I owe you one," he said and suddenly his body began to move.

"What else is new?" she replied, but her heart wasn't in it.

John pushed himself up before the arms reached him. He realized what had happened had taken just a few seconds. He was sure it was all in his mind, and this wasn't really Sam. It was just his mind working things out. He was positive of that, right up until he saw the look on Sam's face and knew it wasn't.

John half crawled/walked to the cellphone and picked it up. Everyone had backed away from him. He straightened himself and put the cellphone up to his ear as he turned to face everyone. Worry covered every face he saw but one. Sam nodded at him to do his thing. John knew it was up to him to save his friend. He had no idea what he was going to do, but in 90% of the things he did, he didn't know what he was going to do until he just did it. He hoped this wasn't one of those times that things didn't work out right.

Chapter 100

"Bruce," John said as calmly as he could. "You better stop what you're doing, or I am going to kill you." John hit the speaker phone button on his cell phone. He wasn't sure it was the best idea, letting them hear what was going on, but he didn't want everyone bothering him about what was happening. "Chet, are you there?" Bruce hit the speaker phone button on Chet's cellphone. Bruce, watching the reflection in the television, nodded at Chet to respond.

"I'm here, John," Chet replied, trying to keep calm. "I'm hurt, but I'm here." Bruce smiled his hideous smile.

"John, I figured you'd be in a ball somewhere, sucking your thumb," Bruce replied from across the city. He wanted Chet to hear John plead for Chet's life. He wanted Chet to think he had a chance. That was when Bruce was going to kill Chet. The moment Chet thought he was getting out of this alive. He was going to snatch all of Chet's hopes and dreams. Not only that, he was going to snatch and destroy the same hope from John. Maybe then, John would crawl back into the bottle where he belonged.

"I think you just made medical history, Bruce," John's voice replied over the cell phone, pulling Bruce away from his warm and fuzzy thoughts. "I believe you managed to cure me of any problems I may have had."

"Face your fears and all that noise?" Bruce asked, amused.

"More like look the devil in the face and spit at him," John retorted.

"Oh, someone grew a backbone," Bruce replied, enjoying himself. "That's good. That's real good. Your buddy here is going to need one, John. You see, I've paralyzed him from the waist down. I've spent my time away studying how to hurt people, how to paralyze people, and how to rip their souls out! That's what I'm going to do, John. I'm going to take apart your little team piece by piece, and then, I'm going to get you. But, not yet. First, I'm going to get that mouthy broad you claim to love so much. I killed your first wife, so why not get number two?" John had glanced over at Jessica during Bruce's tirade. The look on her face was priceless.

"Mouthy?" she whispered. Amanda squeezed her arm in support.

"You touch her, Trip, Amanda, or do anything else to Chet, I am going to rip your arm off and beat you with it," John replied calmly but coldly. John was watching everyone as he spoke. Trip, Jessica, and Amanda were making gestures not to antagonize him, but John's focus was past them. Sam was nodding. John knew what he had to do. He had to get Bruce to focus on John and to get him in such a rage that he forgot about Chet. A team was being sent to Chet's home, but they needed time. John was going to do all he could to give them that time.

"Ohhh," Bruce replied, nearly laughing. "Someone's a little mad. What happened to don't kill? Huh, John? What happened to your precious little code?"

"Sometimes you have to put down a rabid dog, Bruce," John said watching the computer screen Trip had pulled up to track the team. They were still over five minutes away from Chet's. "Everyone knows your nothing more than a rabid dog. Besides, maybe you won, Bruce. Maybe I'm willing to break my code for you. Would that make you happy, Bruce? Would it make you happy to know that you finally won? You couldn't break me by killing my wife, but now, you may have just pushed me over the edge. You may have pushed me past my breaking point, and now, I'm going to kill you, Bruce. You had better come kill me before I find you. Do you understand, Bruce! Huh, do you!" There was laughter from the other end of the phone. For a second, just a split second, John thought maybe he had done it. That was the last time he thought he had the upper hand against Bruce.

Chapter 101

Chet lay on the floor, listening to the entire conversation. He wasn't sure what John was doing. He watched Bruce through the reflection of the television. Bruce pulled the gun from his waistband while he seemed to listen to John. Bruce looked amused.

"John," Chet said, almost in tears. "John, he's got a gun!"

"Did I forget to mention that, John?" Bruce asked, almost giddy. "Did I forget to mention that while your friend is lying here, paralyzed from the waist down, I'm going to blow his brains out?"

"Bruce," John said, trying to get control of the situation but realizing he was close to losing control himself. Bruce grinned at the tone in John's voice. He made sure Chet could see his reflection in the television. Bruce licked the barrel of the gun and giggled. Chet nearly burst out into tears. Chet knew in his mind he was going to die, and there was nothing he could do about it.

"John," Chet was half crying, half whimpering. "John he's going to kill me." Chet began to sob.

"You hear that, John?" Bruce asked softly. "He knows what's going to happen, and he knows there is nothing. Absolutely nothing. That you can do. To stop me."

John looked around the room in a panic. Jessica and Amanda were near tears. Trip was frantically on his phone, pleading. As bad as it looked in the room, John's heart sank when he saw Sam's face, and her hands were clasped together over her mouth, touching her nose.

"No," John whispered. Sam shook her head, almost as if to say it's out of my hands.

"No," John said a little louder.

"John, I'm sorry for everything," Chet cried through the phone.

"You hear that, John?" Bruce asked, almost hysterically. "He's sorry. Do you want to say good-bye, John?"

"No, you do this, and it's over for you, Bruce," John said in a strained voice. He didn't know what else to do. Chet stared at Bruce through the reflection on the television. Tears were in Chet's eyes.

"John, don't you start drinking again! You hear me!" Chet screamed.

"Isn't that sweet?" Bruce said mockingly.

"NO!!!" John screamed. "Not like this! Bruce it's always been about you and me! You come here and get me!"

"You fool," Bruce hissed. "It is about you and me! It's about me destroying everything around you!" Chet was in tears. It was over. As he stared at the reflection at Bruce, Chet thought he saw something move behind Bruce, but it was too dark to be sure. Bruce cocked the gun.

"Bruce!" John screamed.

"What! You worthless piece of trash you still don't get it, do you!?" Bruce was nearly frothing at the mouth. "We play the game by my rules! Not yours! Say good-bye, John! Say good-bye now because I am going to hurt your friend, and then, I'm going to kill him!"

"Good-bye, John," Chet whispered. Chet thought he saw movement again. He strained his eyes against the darkness but couldn't see anything. Chet accepted his fate, shut his eyes, and prayed.

John looked at everyone. Amanda and Jessica were beside themselves, neither one knowing what to do. Trip looked helpless. The computer screen showed the team still over a minute away. A minute they all knew they didn't have. And, then, John saw Sam.

"I'm sorry," Sam said.

"John! Say it now, or he dies!" Bruce screamed. John looked at Sam. She nodded.

"Good-bye, Chet," John said, his voice breaking. Bruce shut his eyes, a feeling of euphoria sweeping through him. Chet squeezed his eyes close and prayed.

"I'm so sorry," he said, crying. "I'm so, so sorry!"

Bruce walked around Chet and kicked him in the back of the head.

"Maybe you won't feel anything now," Bruce said with a sick grin growing on his face.

"Chet!" John screamed. "Bruce, stop!" Bruce kicked Chet in the back of the head twice more. Blood started to pool out of the wound Bruce had opened.

"You still don't get it, John," Bruce screamed. "My game, my rules!"

John just stared at the phone, and then, John heard the sound, that unmistakable, sick sound. After being an FBI agent for as many years as he had, John had lost track of how many gunshots he had heard during his lifetime. Lately, they had all caused him to go into a panic. This time, it didn't. Inside him, something died. Something broke that he hadn't even known had healed. John hadn't felt this way since Mark Glass was killed. John noticed that something had fallen away from his hand. He watched as the cellphone fell from his hand. He thought it was making an awfully loud sound to just be falling through the air.

"That's a gunshot," he murmured, realizing it wasn't the phone making the noise but the gunshot. John turned toward his friends. They were horrified. He looked past them to Sam. She stood there, pain evident in her face. "Take care of him," he murmured again.

"Not yet," she said simply, and looking at him with those haunted eyes, full of pain, she disappeared.

"He's been shot," John said quietly. He looked at everyone, tears flowing down their faces. "He's been shot," he said a little bit louder. Jessica and Chet had been his rocks, and now, one of them was dead.

"Chet," John said, rage filling him. John felt all the emotions he had ever possessed leave his body except for rage. "Chet!" he screamed. John sunk to his knees and looked up at the ceiling.

"CHET!!!!"

The End. . . For Now

Writer's Note:

Yeah, I did it again. When I wrote the writer's note at the end of Book 3, I knew then this moment was coming. I always knew that Bruce would take it personally that Chet shot Bruce, and Bruce would have to have his payback. So now what? Now, John gets even, but not in the way you think.

I can't believe that I've now written 6 of these novels, when not even two years ago, I was struggling just to write one. We have three more novels in this series, and then, well, let's see what happens. I hope you've enjoyed these books as much as I've enjoyed writing them. Now get ready, because as the old saying goes, you ain't seen nuthin' yet!

David

PS. Read on for the short story Bad Day in Queen's Landing!

Bad Day In Queen's Landing

Chapter 1

Chris turned off the TV and shook his head; another Sunday night movie about another cop with issues. Where were the stories about the cops or law enforcement agents that did their jobs without having some kind of personal demon that they had to overcome? Where were the stories of the good men that did their jobs because they were supposed to? Where were the stories about the men that felt they were supposed to make a difference where they lived, so that's where and why they served?

Chris got up and walked across the living room to his kitchen. He looked in the fridge for something cold to drink. He settled on a glass of iced tea. LaCompt County had only become wet a few weeks ago, but Chris had no intention of going wet with it. He didn't like the new law, but his job was to uphold the law, not enforce what he wanted or what he thought was right. Not like his deputy, Cal. Chris shook his head. There were days he wondered why he made Cal his deputy. Chris and Cal Shelby had gone to high school together. Cal had been a couple of grades in front of Chris. They had been friends in high school, and Chris thought he knew Cal, but he had been more wrong than he ever thought possible.

Chris looked down at the file on his kitchen table. He had spent weeks gathering information. He had begun suspecting things months ago, but he never dreamed he would find what he had. The only question was whether to take care of things publicly or privately.

Chris thought he heard something and lifted his head. He was sure he had heard tires on the gravel outside. He walked to the large living room window and lifted the curtain to peer out. It was dark outside, but he thought he saw the silhouette of a SUV. Chris dropped the curtain and retreated back to the kitchen. He kept his service weapon on top of the fridge, but he was heading toward the gun cabinet that held rifles and his shotgun. He opened the case and grabbed the shotgun. The SUV resembled Cal's, but Cal hadn't been out to Chris's in months. Chris also grabbed the rifle and headed back into the living room. He laid the rifle down and slowly lifted the curtain. Chris felt his heart leap into his chest. He was seeing shapes everywhere on his land. There had to be at least 20 men outside, all armed. Chris saw the first muzzle flash and fired the shotgun in response. Gunfire rained through the window and wall in front of him. Chris tried to fall to the ground to protect himself. He felt something rip into his shoulder, thigh, and his side. He laid on the ground and tried to reach for his rifle. He found he couldn't. The front door kicked open, and the last thing Chris saw was the muzzle fire of the weapon the man was holding.

The man stepped over Chris's body, walked into the kitchen, and found the file lying on the kitchen table. He flipped through it for a second. Satisfied, he took the file and headed back outside. He stopped before he headed out the door, turned, and fired one more shot into the body of the local sheriff. The men all got into their SUVs and drove off into the night.

Chapter 2

Cal groaned. He had heard the next door neighbor's rooster "cock-a-doodle-do" for more mornings than he cared to remember. He opened his eyes and saw the sunlight starting to light the room, despite his best efforts to block out the sun coming through the window. Cal sat up and looked at the clock. The red numbers glared back at him. It was already past 6:30. Cal knew he had to get moving. He began his morning procedures. After he had finished his morning rituals and was dressed, he poured his morning energy drink from the big pitcher he kept in his fridge. He looked around the old house. He had bought the place from his parents when they decided the winters were just too cold, and the summers were just too hot in Kentucky. His parents were now living in San Diego where the temperature seemed to never change, regardless of the season.

Cal had spent his entire life in LaCompt County. He graduated from LaCompt County High School and took some classes at the local community college. The county was small, and the main town, Queen's Landing, was even smaller. It was located next to a lake, and tourism helped keep the county afloat. After Chris was elected sheriff, he had approached Cal about being his deputy. Cal had quickly agreed. That had been 10 years ago, and little had changed for Cal. He checked on his folks in California about once a week, checked on his best friend Terrance, or T as he was known, every couple of days, and had breakfast with his sisters a couple of times a week.

This morning was one of those mornings. He was supposed to meet Ann and Carol in town for breakfast in the next five minutes. He was going to be late unless he turned on the sirens and did 90 all the way there. He knew his sisters wouldn't approve of that, but there was a lot Cal did that he was quite sure they wouldn't approve of.

He didn't get to see Ann nearly as much as Carol. Ann was a school teacher and had three children. She had married one of the local boys, Craig, and was happy as could be. Cal was happy for them. Carol, on the other hand, was still single but working as an EMT. Cal saw her constantly on the job. Usually if one of them got a call, so did the other.

Carol had been inspired by their Aunt Charlotte to go into medicine. Charlotte had been one of the best nurses in the state. They had lost her a few years earlier. Cal found it interesting that was about the time things had started to change in his life.

"Change is for the better," he thought to himself. Cal smiled and looked out at his black SUV. He was quite proud of himself. He had been by himself ever since high school, and he was proud of his "investments." He chuckled at his conversation with one of the local bankers yesterday. The banker had wanted to know Cal's secret in investing. Cal had his line ready. "Buy low, sell high," Cal had said to the banker. The banker gave a friendly laugh, but Cal knew it wasn't the answer the banker wanted.

Cal knew he had to get going, or he was going to be really late. He walked outside and had just locked the door when an ambulance pulled up in the driveway. Carol was driving and looked mad. Cal reached in his pocket and pulled out his cellphone. It was off. Cal chuckled. The only way to get service where he lived was to put the phone on a windowsill, put the phone on speaker, and yell at it. Cal normally just turned it off. What could happen in this little town that would be so bad someone needed him 24/7? He was about to find out.

Chapter 3

Carol climbed out of the ambulance with an annoyed look on her face.

"Why don't you have your phone on?" she demanded.

"I can't get a signal, so what's the point?" Cal replied. Cal had been turning on his phone as the exchange took place. He saw numerous missed calls and texts. He nodded, impressed with the amount of calls made trying to locate him. "I take it this isn't over breakfast?" he asked his sister.

"Get in!" Carol demanded. Cal knew that when Carol was like this, there was no arguing with her. Cal locked his seatbelt and prepared to hold on for dear life. Five minutes later, they arrived at their destination, the residence of Chris Rogers's, Cal's boss. Cal looked over at Carol. She gave him her famous "you should have listened to me" look. Cal got out of the ambulance and noticed the front window of the house had been blown out. Bullet holes littered the frame of the house.

"What happened here?" Cal asked quietly. He noticed the mayor walking up toward him. Cal was getting very nervous. The mayor extended his hand, and Cal shook it.

"Cal," the mayor said crisply. "As of right now, you're the new sheriff of LaCompt County. We'll deal with things later, but right now, you need to figure out who killed Chris and quickly." The mayor nodded curtly, turned, and walked away. The reporter for the local paper came up to Cal.

"Anything I can do, Cal?" Tyler, the reporter asked.

"Not right now, Tyler," Cal replied. "When did this happen?"

"No one knows for sure," Tyler replied. "People started trying to call Chris this morning; that was the only way anyone figured out something was wrong."

"No one heard the gun shots?" Cal exclaimed.

"The only neighbor around is 80, and she can't hear you if you yell directly in her ear," Tyler replied. Cal shook his head. Kentucky Highway Patrol had shown up and had offered to help process the scene. Cal knew that meant they were going to take over the investigation, which was fine with him. What had happened here? Cal looked around and saw his brother-in-law, Craig. Craig waved him over, and Cal headed toward him.

"Bad day in Queen's Landing," Craig said. Cal nodded. He hadn't gone inside the house yet because he didn't want to see his dead friend. Cal was looking over toward some tire tracks that had been roped off. Cal motioned with his head for Craig to follow him.

"Any chance you recognize these tire tracks?" Cal asked. Cal didn't have a clue about cars, tires, trucks, or anything motorized. Craig looked for a second at the tracks and then back at Cal. There was a confused look on his face.

"Yeah, I recognize them," Craig replied. "Don't you?" Cal shook his head no. "Man, those are the same type of treads your SUV makes." Cal nearly broke his neck as he whipped his head around to look at Craig. Cal had a bad feeling about where this was going.

"Am I the only person that has those type of tire treads?" Cal asked, never looking at Craig.

"No," Craig responded, shaking his head. "They look like they belong to those SUVs that Hernandez's creeps roll around in." Cal was torn. On one hand, he was thrilled that there were other vehicles than his that made the tracks. On the other, he had rather it was anyone other than Hernandez. Hernandez Marrero was the known marijuana king of LaCompt County. There were questions as to whether or not he was involved with the Mexican drug cartel. Cal didn't think so. He thought Hernandez helped spread those rumors so others would be scared to cross him. Regardless if the stories were true or not, no one crossed Hernandez. Cal thanked Craig for the help and started for the house. Craig watched Cal walk away. Craig shook his head. Cal may have been a smart man, but there were times that Craig wondered if he had any common sense. If the stories were true about Cal, he was the dumbest man in the county for the deal he had made.

Chapter 4

Cal walked into the house and nearly threw up. He had seen crime scenes before, but this was absolutely senseless. Cal counted five bullet holes, minimum, in Chris. He nodded, and Carol dropped the cover back over Chris. Since the county was so small, Carol had become deputy coroner. For the most part, she took care of crime scenes and brought the bodies back to the coroner, unless an emergency call came in, and she was needed somewhere else.

Carol walked with Cal through the house, trying to make sure he didn't get sick and contaminate the crime scene. She looked especially irritated with him today. Cal stopped and turned toward her.

"Have I done something that makes you more irritated with me than usual?" Cal asked. Carol gave Cal a dirty look.

"What do you think happened here?" she asked very angrily.

"I have no idea, Carol," Cal responded, genuinely confused. Carol turned and studied him for a minute. She pursed her lips and nodded.

"This was senseless," Carol said quietly. Cal nodded. "It makes me angry. I'm sorry if I took it out on you." Cal reached out and hugged his sister with one arm. Cal noticed something and let her go. Carol followed Cal, watching him.

"Guys," Cal called toward the crime scene techs. They came to where Cal was. Carol saw it. There was a blood trail that led from the front door into the kitchen. The trail then led from the kitchen back the way it came and out the front door. Cal went and stood where the drops pooled in the kitchen.

"Was there something on the table?" Carol asked. Cal turned toward her, nodding.

"I think so," Cal replied. "Apparently, someone came in here to get something and then left. The question is, whose blood dripped? Chris's, or one of his assailants'?" Cal turned toward one of the techs who was smiling.

"Don't even start on us, man," the tech said. "You've watched too much TV if you think you'll get this blood analyzed in under 24 hours." Cal didn't say a word; he just stepped back and let his sister bite the man's head off.

"That is an officer down," Carol said, pointing at Chris's body. "Does that not light a fire under you?" The tech gulped and turned toward his supervisor who just nodded and left the room.

"I'm sorry, ma'am," the tech said. "I'll personally put a rush on it." The man left, and Cal found himself chuckling. Carol turned around with an amused smirk on her face.

"What are you laughing about?" she asked. Cal shook his head. There was no way in the world he was answering that question. He continued to work the crime scene. Craig offered to give Cal a lift home so he could get his vehicle and begin his investigation. Cal accepted, and shortly after, he was on the road.

After about 10 minutes of driving, Cal pulled up to Hernandez's known hangout. One of his goons met Cal outside. He led Cal inside. Hernandez nodded at Cal as he entered the room. Hernandez got up and went to his safe. Cal noticed a wrap on Hernandez's arm and wondered if that could be the cause of the blood Cal had seen at the crime scene. Hernandez picked up an envelope and handed it to Cal. Cal opened it and saw the five grand he had been expecting. Cal smiled at his return on his investment. He sat down and looked Hernandez right in the eye.

"What were you doing at the sheriff's house last night?" Cal asked. He had steeled himself for the response he was sure he was about to hear.

The four goons of Hernandez pulled their guns on Cal. As he heard their weapons click, for the first time in the past 10 years, Cal wondered if he was making a mistake by taking payoffs from Hernandez to look the other way as he sold weed in LaCompt County.

Chapter 5

"Who says I was at the sheriff's house last night?" Hernandez asked.

"Come on, Hernandez," Cal replied. "My brother-in-law could tell the tire tracks came from vehicles like yours. Do you think everyone in this town is stupid enough not to figure it out?"

Hernandez laughed. "Yeah, I do," he replied.

Cal was seriously beginning to think he had made a mistake. He thought about the conversation he had had with his sister a few months ago, regarding Hernandez. The rumor had been that Hernandez wasn't just selling in LaCompt County, and he wasn't just selling weed. Carol had told him that cocaine use and heroin use were up tremendously in the surrounding counties. She had also heard that the Mexican drug cartel was supposedly interested in making some deals with Hernandez.

Cal was beginning to suspect that Hernandez wasn't honoring their agreement. There was something else that bothered Cal. LaCompt County wasn't that big. There was only a population of around 15,000 people. How was Hernandez making enough to pay Cal $5,000.00 every two months and still be making the money he was obviously making? As Cal glanced around at all the guns pointed in his direction, he decided that this might not be the best time to ask that question to Hernandez.

"Hernandez, do I need to do something, or not?" Cal asked. Hernandez frowned. "I can't do what you paid me to do if I don't know what's going on." Hernandez signaled for his guys to lower their guns. He leaned in angrily.

"If you'd done your job, we wouldn't have had to take care of the sheriff," Hernandez said in a low voice.

"What do you mean?" Cal asked. Hernandez said nothing, stood up, strode over to a table, and picked up a file for Cal to see.

"This buried both of us," he continued. "Now, go do the job I'm paying you for!" Cal thought about saying something else, but thought better of it. He left. Just before, he exited the door he turned back.

"Is there anything going on I need to know about?" he asked Hernandez. Hernandez barked a laugh.

"No, there's nothing you need to know," Hernandez answered, emphasizing need. Cal turned, walked out to his vehicle, started it, and took off, knowing this was probably the last time he would see Hernandez on friendly terms.

Chapter 6

Cal walked into Terrance's house. Knocking was useless. Terrance never answered the door. He also never locked the door. When Cal walked in, he had to hold his breath while searching for Terrance. Smoke filled the home. Cal found Terrance taking a hit off a bong. Terrance raised his hand at him in greeting, stoned out of his mind. Cal grabbed Terrance and drug him out the back door to fresh air. Terrance was bigger than Cal. Terrance used to be a standout middle linebacker in high school. He used to be 6'2", 215 lbs. and could run a 4.4 forty. Terrance had joined the military out of high school and had become a firearms and marksman expert. Cal had never gotten the full story, but somewhere in the Middle East, Terrance was either shot or stepped on something and severely injured his leg. He didn't lose it or anything like that, but he could always tell when bad weather was coming, and it did seem to legitimately hurt on a consistent basis. Terrance now spent his days smoking pot and claiming it was all medicinal marijuana, forgetting the fact that Kentucky didn't recognize medicinal marijuana.

"What's eatin' you?" Terrance asked.

"I think Hernandez killed Chris," Cal replied solemnly. "I think it's all my fault."

"Chris? The sheriff?" Terrance asked. "Man, either I'm more stoned than I realized, or Hernandez just stepped up his game." Terrance looked over at his friend who didn't know what to do. "Chris finally figure out you're taking money from Hernandez?" Cal looked over at Terrance in shock.

"T, how did you know?" Cal asked.

"Do you think we're all stupid?" Terrance asked in response. "You're rolling in money that you shouldn't have. You have never brought in any of his men, and every time one of them gets popped, they suddenly get out because of mishandling of evidence. I'm stoned, not stupid. The question is, what did Chris have that Hernandez killed him over?"

"Chris had some type of file apparently," Cal answered, still shocked that Terrance had figured things out.

"What are you going to do?" Terrance asked.

"I don't know what I can do," Cal admitted. "If I take him down, he'll turn in the file. If I try and take it, he'll kill me."

"You deputies are a bunch of wimps," Terrance said, shaking his head in disgust.

"I'm sheriff now!" Cal spat back. "Besides who are you to talk?" Terrance lifted an eyebrow and looked down at his leg. Cal looked a little ashamed of himself for blowing up at his friend like that. Terrance sighed and crossed his arms. He knew how to fix this mess; he didn't want to, but he knew how.

"How many men does Hernandez have?" Terrance asked.

"I have no idea, no more than 8 to 10 at a time are at his safe house," Cal replied. Terrance nodded, and walked inside; Cal followed. Terrance walked up to a wall, took a look at Cal, and made up his mind.

"You've looked the other way on the things, so I do for a long time, guess I owe you," Terrance said and began to shove a book case. Cal shook his head, thinking Terrance was stoned out of his mind. He was shocked when he heard a creak. The bookcase moved back to reveal a stairway. Cal looked at Terrance in awe.

"I may have been a slightly bigger deal than I let on when I was in the military," Terrance said as an explanation.

"I'll say," Cal muttered. "I'll say."

Chapter 7

Terrance led Cal downstairs to what Cal could only call an armory. There were guns and ammo everywhere. Shelves, display cases, and hooks on the walls all held guns of every kind. There were crates holding bullets everywhere.

"Expecting a zombie attack?" Cal asked. Terrance looked at Cal like he was stupid.

"Let's just say I'm ready in case I ever need to be, for anything," Terrance answered.

"T, you have more ordinance here than we do," Cal said, still surveying the room.

"I'm better trained than you, too," Terrance replied. Cal slowly turned to Terrance.

"Why are you showing me this?" Cal asked.

"I said I owe you," Terrance replied.

"So you're going to loan me ammunition and weapons to take down Hernandez?" Cal asked, hoping that was the answer but fearing it wasn't.

"Yeah," Terrance answered, picking up an automatic rifle and beginning to load a clip into it.

"Is that all?" Cal asked. Terrance gave Cal an annoyed look.

"What do you want from me?" Terrance asked. "Do you want me to hold hands with you and sing Kumbaya? Or, would you rather I strap up and we go run Hernandez and his boys out of town?" Terrance gave a challenging glare at Cal, waiting for his answer. Cal ran his hand through his hair and looked around the room. He looked back at Terrance.

"I can't," Cal responded. Terrance looked at Cal flatly. "You're not a deputy." Terrance barked a laugh, but Cal's face never changed.

"You're serious!" Terrance said, more than asked. Cal slowly nodded.

"If we do this, then people will get killed, and I can't protect you," Cal answered. "If you were deputized, then we might, and I mean, MIGHT, get away with it." Terrance stuck his tongue into his bottom lip, thinking. He slowly nodded.

"Do it," Terrance said.

"Do what?" Cal asked, not believing what he was hearing.

"Deputize me," Terrance answered.

"You cannot be serious," Cal said, not believing what he was hearing. Terrance was grabbing more guns from around the room.

"You heard me. Deputize me," Terrance answered. "I'm more than qualified. In fact, I'm probably overqualified." Cal had never seen his friend like this since high school. Terrance looked so alive.

"What happened to you over there?" Cal asked quietly. Terrance stopped in mid-movement with his back to Cal. Terrance's face tightened. He never looked at Cal.

"Some things are better not known," Terrance answered. "Let's just say the same guy didn't come back."

"Are you sure about this, T?" Cal asked. Terrance didn't answer for a second. "You don't have to do this, T," Cal said softly, knowing he would never survive this without his friend. It didn't matter to Cal; he couldn't ask his friend to do this. Terrance remained facing away from Cal.

"Some things are worth fighting for," Terrance answered. "You done taking dirty money?"

"Yes," Cal answered quietly. Terrance nodded and turned to Cal.

"Then let's strap up, get me deputized, and put these punks out of business," Terrance said with a gleam in his eye that Cal had never seen before. "I can't stand drug runners."

"You smoke marijuana," Cal replied. Terrance looked at him like he was crazy, shook his head, and started up the stairs.

"It's for a medical condition," Terrance replied as he headed upstairs, leaving Cal by himself.

"I swear, I am never going to understand that man," Cal said to himself.

Chapter 8

As they came up the stairs, Cal put his hand down to his service weapon. He heard rustling upstairs and was afraid Hernandez had sent one of his boys to take Cal out. When he came out of the stairwell, there stood Carol.

"Did you play basketball this week?" Carol was asking Terrance. "It smells like it."

"I have a prescription," Terrance replied. Carol rolled her eyes, looked at her brother, and then back at Terrance and the ordinance they were carrying.

"Going hunting, boys?" Carol asked.

"For Hernandez's men," Terrance answered. Carol looked surprised. She turned toward Cal for verification, and Cal nodded. Carol nodded slowly, shrugged, and headed down the stairwell without a word.

"Did she know what was down there?" Cal asked. Terrance nodded. "How does she know what's going on down there, and I didn't?"

"You're the fuzz," Terrance answered simply.

"I'm your friend and knew you were smoking pot and didn't say anything!" Cal exclaimed. Terrance turned around and looked Cal straight in the eye.

"You're a dirty cop," Terrance explained. "I didn't know if you'd try to blackmail me, turn me in, or just let it ride." Cal's mouth was open in shock. It remained open as he saw Carol bring up two bullet-proof vests and a rifle with a scope on it. Terrance started to say something, but Carol cut him off.

"You can't lay cover fire and help him take the place," Carol said. Terrance thought, nodded, and turned toward Cal.

"How long will it take you to deputize her?" Terrance asked. Cal shook his head.

"Nope, no way!" he exclaimed. Carol gave Cal the "don't be an idiot" look.

"You know Dad taught me how to shoot," Carol said.

"If you get shot or worse, Dad will kill me," Cal replied.

"I'm simply laying down cover fire," Carol said. Cal couldn't believe the mess he had gotten himself in. "Besides," she continued. "Someone's got to help you two. You can't shoot, and he's half-baked." Terrance looked up from what he was doing, started to argue, realized Carol was right, shrugged, and continued to load his weapon.

"What are you even doing here?" Cal asked, trying to get some control of this situation. Carol looked at Cal very angrily.

"I came to tell you that Becky that you went to high school with is dead. Heroin." Cal didn't say anything; he just looked down at the floor. When he looked up, Terrance and Carol were staring at him, not sure whether to be mad at Cal or not.

"Come on," he said quietly. "Let's go to my office ,so I can figure out how to deputize you two." Cal turned and left the house without another word.

"Try not to let him get killed," Carol said quietly to Terrance.

"I know. He's your brother," Terrance responded. Carol shook her head.

"That's not why," Carol replied, grabbing the rifle and heading out of the house. "I'm still not sure I don't want to kill him."

Chapter 9

Cal's legs were hurting from squatting behind his hiding place. It was close to midnight, and most of the activity had died down at Hernandez's house. There were only six goons Cal had counted. The three had decided to make sure they got Hernandez. Cal told them the drug trade had to end, regardless if he got back the file on himself or not.

"Do you know what the signal is supposed to be?" Terrance asked Cal. Cal shook his head. "Cal, it's dark out here. I can't see you if you're nodding or shaking your head!"

"I don't have a clue," Cal admitted. "I did see Carol sneak over there a few minutes ago and then go back to her hiding spot."

"Where?" Terrance asked. Cal got his hand as close to Terrance's face as he could and pointed where he had seen her. "Oh, that's good."

"What's good?" Cal asked. It was at that time he saw a trail of fire head toward the direction Cal had pointed at seconds ago. He peered into the night and noticed there were a couple of drums there. They appeared to have some symbols on them. "Is that gasoline?"

That was the last thing Cal heard for a while except for the loud explosion that took out the drums, vehicles, and part of the house.

A few seconds later, a few goons stormed out of the house with weapons. Cal watched one of them drop and realized from the angle of the bullet entry he had seen, it hadn't come from him or Terrance. His sister was picking off the men! The second fell, and Cal had an internal count going. There were six goons and Hernandez by his count, so now, they were down to five men total. Gunshots filled the night air, and Terrance and Cal got separated during the fire fight. After a few minutes, Cal was pretty sure they had taken down four of the six goons. Cal made his way into the house as stealthily as he could. He could see movement in the kitchen. There were two men firing out the kitchen window at Terrance's general direction. Cal came around the corner quietly and realized that Hernandez was one of the men. He aimed very carefully and prepared to squeeze the trigger when something slammed into his chest, knocking him down and the gun from his hand. He looked up, the breath knocked out of his body, at the other goon he hadn't accounted for.

The bullet had hit Cal in his Kevlar vest, but Cal was pretty sure he had broken a rib. Hernandez walked over and made a gesture for the goon to head into the kitchen. Cal heard a sharp crack and the sound of someone hitting the floor, Hernandez didn't seem to notice; he was staring at Cal.

"You think you can come in here and take me out after everything I did for you?" Hernandez asked threateningly. Cal heard another sharp crack. He heard a moan from inside the kitchen. Hernandez aimed his gun at Cal's forehead.

"I should have done this the same night I took down the sheriff," Hernandez said. Cal closed his eyes and began to pray. He heard a gun go off but didn't feel anything. He waited just a second and heard something fall.

"But, you didn't, and I just took you out!" Terrance exclaimed. Cal opened his eyes and saw Hernandez lying on the ground, looking toward him with a bullet hole in his head. Cal gulped. Terrance came over and helped Cal up. Cal held onto a table, to keep himself upright. Terrance disappeared into the house. Carol appeared in the doorway.

"You okay?" Carol asked. Cal nodded. He didn't trust himself to speak. He was afraid his voice would crack from the terror. He felt something shoved into his hands. Terrance handed him the folder that Chris had compiled on him. Cal took a deep breath and handed it back to Terrance.

"You two decide what to do with it," Cal said.

"You realize this could ruin you?" Terrance asked.

"T, I have messed up bad, and it's time I pay," Cal responded. Terrance looked at Carol. She nodded. Terrance reached into his pocket, pulled out a lighter, and tossed the file into an empty sink. He lit the folder, stood there, and watched it burn.

"You owe both of us," Carol said as she watched it burn. Cal nodded. "You can start by being a good sheriff, the kind of sheriff this county needs." Cal nodded again. Carol sighed and waved him toward her. "Come on, let's get those ribs looked at."

Epilogue

Over the next few days, life went back to normal for Cal. He deputized Terrance and told him that he had to quit smoking marijuana. He was pretty sure Terrance was stoned when he told him. A new girl, Samantha, moved to Queen's Landing and seemed to flirt with Cal any chance she got. Carol continued to keep an eye on Cal to make sure he was on the straight and narrow.

It was a few weeks later that Cal woke up in the middle of the night and felt someone in the room. He started to reach for his weapon on the nightstand when he heard a gun being cocked.

"It's not there," a voice said. "I know who you are and what you did, and I'm not happy about it. Hernandez was an idiot, but he's my idiot. You had no right to kill him. I'm going to kill you Mr. Shelby...just not tonight." With that, Cal felt, more than saw, the intruder leave the room. Cal didn't sleep the rest of the night. The next morning, at the sheriff's office, Cal told Terrance what had happened.

"What are you going to do?" Terrance asked.

"I'm going to do what I promised you two I'd do," Cal answered. "We're going to start by cleaning up what's left of the Hernandez mess." Terrance nodded and went over to the weapons locker. "What are you doing?"

"I'm not going out there to fight them barehanded," Terrance said, tossing Cal a shotgun.

"T, this is my mess, and I wouldn't dare ask you to help," Cal replied.

"That's good," Terrance said, checking his weapon. He looked up, and Cal stood there still in shock. "If you try and hug me or something, I will shoot you."

Cal nodded, and the two headed out the door.

"Thanks, T," Cal said as they got in the vehicle.

"Don't mention it," Terrance replied. "I mean it, don't mention it again."

The two took off in the car to begin the long road of cleaning up the mess Cal had made.